W9-ANQ-002

WHY DID THE DINOSAURS DISAPPEAR?

WHY DID THE DINOSAURS DISAPPEAR?

Questions about life in the past answered by
Dr Philip Whitfield with the
Natural History Museum

Viking

VIKING
Published by the Penguin Group
Viking Penguin Inc., 375 Hudson Street, New York, 10014, U.S.A.
Penguin Books Ltd, 27 Wrights Lane, London W8 5TZ, England.
Penguin Books Australia Ltd, Ringwood, Victoria, Australia.
Penguin Books Canada Ltd, 2801 John Street, Markham, Ontario,
Canada L3R 1B4.
Penguin Books (N.Z.) Ltd, 182–190 Wairau Road, Auckland 10,
New Zealand.

Penguin Books Ltd, Registered Offices:
Harmondsworth, Middlesex, England.

First published in 1991 by Viking Penguin,
a division of Penguin Books U.S.A.

Why Did the Dinosaurs Disappear?
was conceived, edited and designed by
Marshall Editions
170 Piccadilly
London W1V 9DD

Copyright © Marshall Editions Developments Limited, 1991
All rights reserved

Editor
Carole McGlynn

Art Editor
Daphne Mattingly

Picture Research
Richard Philpott

Managing Editor
Ruth Binney

Production
Barry Baker
Janice Storr
Nikki Ingram

Library of Congress catalog card number: 90-50993
(CIP data available)

ISBN 0-670-84055-6

Printed and bound in Portugal
by Printer Portuguesa

10 9 8 7 6 5 4 3 2 1

Without limiting the rights under copyright reserved above, no
part of this publication may be reproduced, stored in or
introduced into a retrieval system, or transmitted, in any form
or by any means (electronic, mechanical, photocopying, recording
or otherwise), without the prior written permission of both the
copyright owner and the above publisher of this book.

Contents

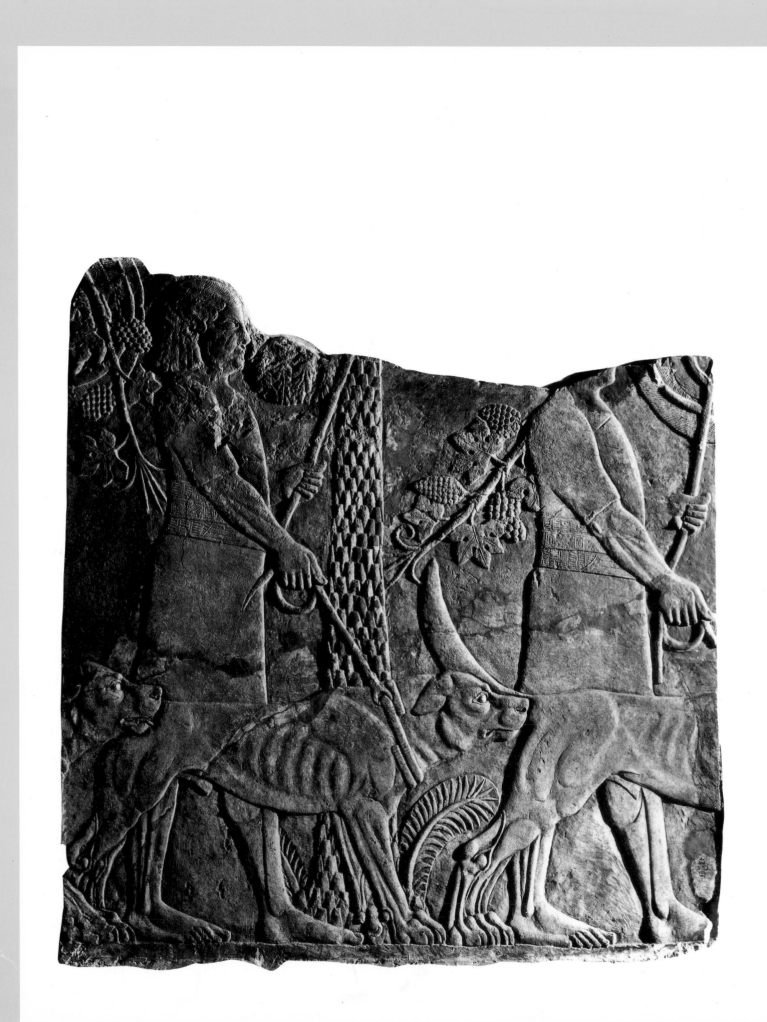

Introduction

The story of the past is much more than a series of dates; it is an intriguing tale of exciting developments that created the world we know today, and will just as certainly shape one of the many possible futures that lie ahead.

In *Why Did the Dinosaurs Disappear?* we travel on a marvelous time journey and witness the fascinating events that make up the history of our planet. The story started dramatically, 16 billion years ago, with an explosion called the Big Bang, which gave birth to time, space, and the whole Universe. And it continues with the extraordinary unfolding of the events that have built our planetary home – the Earth – with its seas, its atmosphere, and its ever-shifting continents.

Once the world was inhabited, the planet changed forever, as living things began their amazing, never-ending game of variations called evolution. The main stages in that game are set down here, and reveal how many different sorts of creatures, including fish, amphibians, reptiles, birds, and mammals, came into being, flourished, and then died out, throughout the ages. Most remarkable of all the animals that roamed the ancient Earth were the dinosaurs, which ruled the planet for over 100 million years before they, too, disappeared in one of the great mysteries of the past. The dinosaurs included in their members some of the most awesome beasts that roamed the planet – from the fearsome meat-eating *Tyrannosaurus*, more than 50 feet (26 meters) long, to the plant-eaters, gentle giants up to 70 feet (21 meters) from head to tail.

About three million years ago, our ancestors walked the Earth and began evolving into humans. To help understand the story of our past, the book answers questions about our complicated family tree, and traces the ways in which our ancestors began to talk, tamed fire, made more and more complex tools, and gradually spread over the whole world. It looks at how ancient people first became farmers, how they built huts, and progressed to building houses, then cities.

A journey back in time poses intriguing questions about our origins. In the pages that follow, the answers to many of them bring the ancient past vividly to life.

When did time begin?

Just as the future stretches for ever in front of us, it seems that the past goes backward without stopping behind us. If this were so, time would have no beginning.

But all the clues that scientists have collected point to the astonishing fact that everything in the Universe—including time itself—had a single, once and for all, beginning. The beginning of time, which has been called the "Big Bang," happened about 16 billion years ago—that is, 16,000,000,000 years in the past. Before the Big Bang nothing existed, not even time.

The Big Bang was an incredibly violent explosion. In it everything came into being as an expanding ball of pure energy. The fireball of the explosion was fantastically hot and very small. But from the beginning it started to get bigger, and to cool down. When the explosion had spread and cooled enough, tiny particles began to form. These soon got together to form atoms, the material of which all things are made—gases, rocks, even human bodies.

Even now, because of Big Bang, the Universe is continuing to get bigger and the energy from the explosion is still everywhere in space. Astronomers can still pick up and measure this energy using sensitive radio telescopes. And through powerful telescopes, distant objects in the Universe can be seen moving away from us at speeds close to the speed of light.

How old are the stars?

The stars are younger than the Universe. When the Universe began 16 billion years ago it contained no stars. It consisted simply of huge amounts of gas that were expanding and getting cooler all the time. This gas was probably all hydrogen, the simplest element. It seems, though, that there was more gas in some parts of the Universe than others, so that in some places huge clouds of gas slowly clumped together under the influence of gravity.

After another three billion years—that is about 13 billion years ago—some of these huge masses of gas began to turn into galaxies. Each galaxy contained enough material or matter to create billions of stars like our own Sun.

Stars were made as the atoms of hydrogen started joining together. This joining created incredible amounts of energy and explains why stars—including our own Sun—are so hot.

The Andromeda galaxy, a giant spiral galaxy 2.2 million light-years away from Earth.

An artist's impression of the impact of the Big Bang, 16 billion years ago (left).

How old is our planet?

It is likely that our Sun and all of the planets around it—the Solar System—were formed at about the same time, that is between four and a half and five billion years ago. As the cloud of gas and dust that collapsed to form the Sun did so, it changed in appearance from a ball-like shape to a spinning flattened disk with a central bulge.

The bulge became the Sun and the whirling gas and dust in the disk clustered into larger and larger bodies of material that eventually became planets. One of them, the third planet out from the Sun, was our own planet Earth.

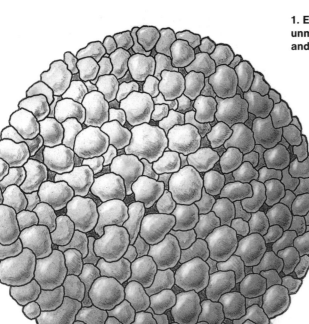

1. Early Earth: a cluster of unmelted lumps of rock, dust, and metals.

2. At a later stage in the Earth's formation the core has melted and a rocky crust has formed.

Asteroid hitting the young Earth

How has the Earth changed since it was made?

Almost every part of the Earth has been changing since the time it was made around four and a half billion years ago. The Earth started as a great jumbled mixture of lumps of rock, metal, and dust. The lumps clustered together, but every so often other lumps, large and small, from the cloud disk around the Sun crashed into the young planet, smashed the part they hit and as they did so added new materials from out in space.

The crucial change early on in the Earth's history was caused by heat. At that time the Earth was working rather like a nuclear power station—it was breaking down materials like uranium and making huge amounts of heat. In a lump of matter as big as the Earth, all this heat could not escape into space and much of it remained trapped inside the planet, and caused the "meltdown" of most of the Earth.

So from those early days on, most of the inside of our planet has been made of hot, liquid metals and rock. Of the core, only the middle is solid. The lightest, most heat-resistant parts of the Earth rose to the surface and made its solid crust, but the Earth's crust was probably never a single, unbroken sheet of rock. It consisted of separate sections or "plates."

These plates do not stay still. They were (and still are) being extended at their edges wherever new molten rock rises to the surface and solidifies. One plate can also slip under the edge of the one next to it and get so hot that it turns back into molten rock. The process by which these rock plates move about and change is called "plate tectonics."

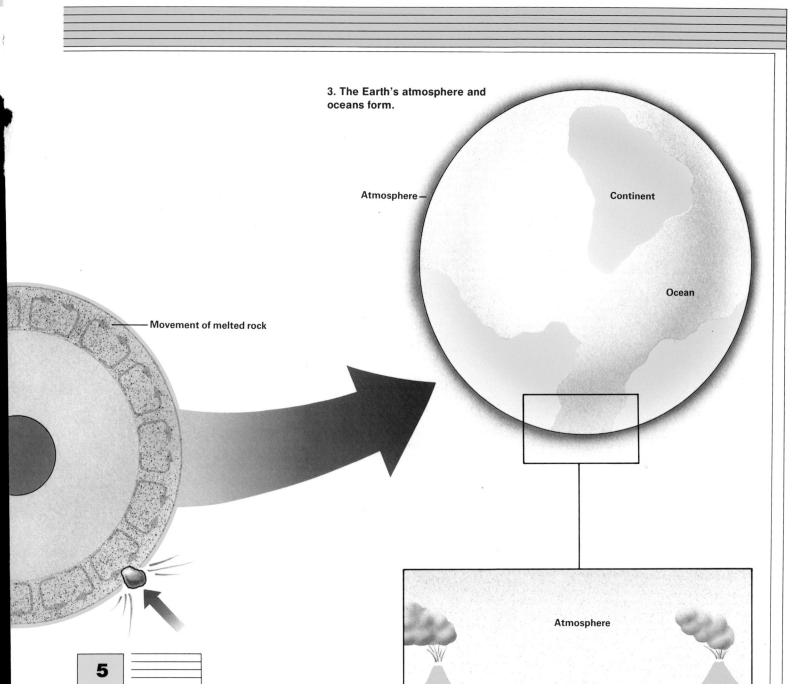

3. The Earth's atmosphere and oceans form.

Atmosphere—

Continent

Ocean

—Movement of melted rock

Atmosphere

Ocean

New crust forming

Molten rock

5

When were oceans made?

In the young Earth, wherever new molten rock came to the surface, volcanoes erupted. The mixture of gases and fumes sent out from the volcanoes formed the beginnings of Earth's atmosphere, which probably contained the gases nitrogen, carbon dioxide, and water vapor.

The water vapor eventually produced clouds. From these clouds the first rain fell, and began to make the oceans of the world. And it is here that all life began. By washing out minerals from the rocks it passed over, the pure rain water carried salts into the oceans. So from the time they began, around four billion years ago, the oceans have been getting ever saltier.

Both the air around us and the seas encircling our continents first came out of the ground as gases and vapor from volcanoes. Each of the rocky plates of the crust gets partially extended at the edges, as molten rock from beneath cools and solidifies.

Over millions of years, the power of water and winds has slowly broken down the solid rocks of the Earth's crust. The fine particles of rock produced in this way (sediment) were washed into the seas, where they sank to the bottom. Here, this sand or mud was slowly pressed down by more sediment and eventually formed layers of rock, known as sedimentary rocks.

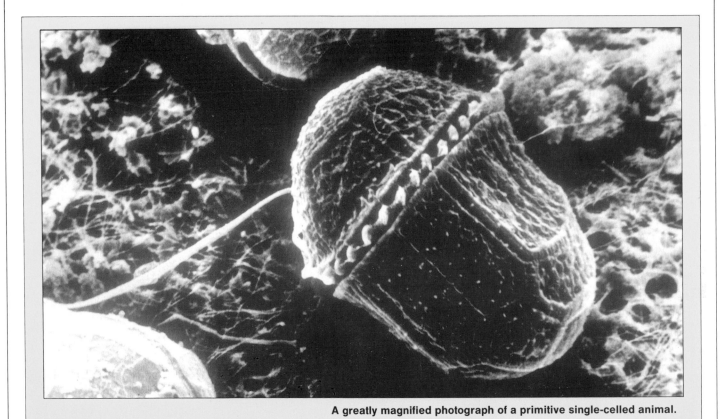

A greatly magnified photograph of a primitive single-celled animal.

How did life begin?

This is a question that no scientist can pretend to be able to answer completely. Most scientists, though, feel that they know when life first started on Earth, and have some ideas about how it was organized.

No life at all was possible on the early Earth before there were seas. However, less than 1,000 million years after the solid crust first formed, the seas contained minute forms of life. Microscopic fossils are preserved in sea-bed rocks over 3,500 million years old. These fossils seem to be sea-dwelling creatures each made up of a single living unit—a single cell. They were like the microscopic organisms called bacteria that we know today.

Since there was no oxygen in the air or seas at that time, these early living things, unlike most living things today, must have been able to live without oxygen.

At some point between the formation of the seas and the first appearance of simple cells, then, life must have had its beginnings. It is thought that life developed as clusters of molecules in the sea, all containing the element carbon. Gradually, these molecules became more complex, until they were able to make copies of themselves. Once they could do that they were really alive and the evolution of life could begin.

By 3,200 million years ago, the first plantlike bacteria, called blue-green algae, had evolved. They could trap sunlight and carbon dioxide from the air and use them to make new living material in the vital process called photosynthesis. A waste product of photosynthesis is oxygen and the levels of oxygen in the Earth's air began to increase. This change probably triggered the evolution of a range of new, more complex living things, including plants and animals. These new animals needed oxygen to live and breathe, and they give off carbon dioxide as waste. So these animals could only have appeared on Earth after the plants had released enough oxygen into the atmosphere.

7

Could life have come from space?

A small group of scientists, including the British astronomer Sir Fred Hoyle, believe that life began off our planet and came to Earth "ready-made" in the form of inactive spores, or seeds.

Their idea is that life developed among the stars, in the complicated particles in the gas and dust of space. Life on our planet is supposed to have begun when these drifted down to Earth, possibly spread by comet tails. Sir Fred Hoyle thinks that this also explains the outbreak of plagues on Earth, such as the Black Death and Bubonic Plague, and of diseases such as influenza. Most scientists think that these ideas cannot be true.

8

Can life be created in the laboratory?

Scientists can use experiments to discover much about the origins of life—but cannot yet re-create life itself.

At present it cannot. Although today's scientists can make in a laboratory the parts of a very simple living thing such as a virus, they cannot piece them together into something that is truly alive.

In the laboratory, what scientists can do is to re-create what they think went on in the Earth's atmosphere *before* life began. The complex chemicals needed to make living things were probably made in the damp air of ancient Earth by the action of lightning, and perhaps also of powerful ultraviolet rays from the Sun. We can try to mimic these processes in a laboratory.

If strong electric sparks are shot through sealed containers which hold a mixture of water vapor, nitrogen, and carbon dioxide (the gases in ancient air), a complicated mixture of life molecules is found in the tarry liquid that gradually builds up in the container over time.

In today's seas, such substances would immediately be absorbed as food by tiny creatures. But before life began, these substances built up in the shallow seas into a thin "soup." Probably, the first living things were made from the chemicals in this "soup."

What were the earliest animals like?

The many creatures that lived nearly a billion years ago in the Precambrian time included true animals. They moved about and ate and had young. Their bodies, though, were so soft that they quickly rotted after the animals died.

Because fossils are usually formed from the hard parts of an animal, we have almost no idea what these creature really looked like when they were alive. Often the only remains of them are tracks and burrows in mud or sand which have been turned to rock.

The earliest animals that can be described in detail come from an age when the sea was bursting with animal life. At this time, around 500 million years ago, an explosion of new animal life forms took place. Many of these animals grew "hard parts"—that is, shells, scales, or other types of protective body armor. These hard parts, because they could be preserved in the rock, produced the first fossils to show any detail of the creatures' bodies.

During this time, which was called the Cambrian Age, examples of almost all the major types of sea animals without backbones that live today were produced. There were sponges, corals, and many different kinds of worms. There were also very many types of arthropods—these are animals with a skeleton on the outside, jointed limbs, and a segmented body. They include today's insects, spiders, scorpions, crabs, and shrimp.

Where can their remains be seen?

The remains of these creatures can be found in many places on Earth, but the best ones of all are those found in the Burgess Shale in western Canada.

These fossils were first discovered in 1909 by a man who was then America's most famous fossil hunter, Charles Dolittle Walcott. He collected tens of thousands of specimens in the fine-grained shale and began describing them. But he assumed that these fossil animals belonged to the same main groups that exist today. He missed the exciting fact that the Burgess Shale animals included not only most modern groups without backbones, but also dozens of hitherto unknown creatures which have no living "look-alikes."

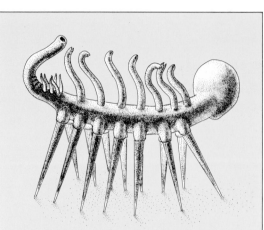

One of the weirdest of the strange Burgess Shale animals was *Hallucigenia*. Only about 1 in (2 cm) long, it had seven pairs of spines, seven tentacles, a rounded "head," and a tube-shaped tail.

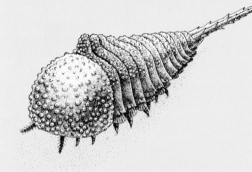

Habelia was an early arthropod from the Burgess Shale. Its head bore short antennae. Behind that were six pairs of branched legs with which it was able to walk in the mud.

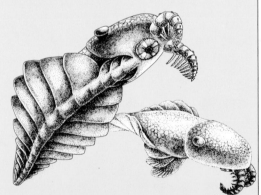

Anomalocaris was the "great white shark" of the Cambrian seas. It navigated with its huge eyes and grasped its prey with two large catching arms at its front in order to place the food in its mouth like a circular nutcracker.

When and how did they live?

The first of these animals that can be described in good detail lived between 590 and 505 million years ago. The dramatic explosion in the number of different sorts of animals took place at the beginning of that time, during the Cambrian Age. The Burgess Shale animals were alive roughly halfway through this time span, about 530 million years ago.

The Burgess Shale animals lived in quite shallow seawater and moved about on mud banks along the base of a large marine reef. This reef was not built by reef-constructing corals as it would be today, since such corals did not exist 530 million years ago. Instead, reefs at that far distant time were built by tiny seaweedlike plants (algae) that could make hard skeletons encrusted with lime in the way that corals do today.

It was massive mud flows down the reef face that produced for us the amazingly lucky chance of the Burgess Shale fossils.

The flows pushed whole collections of living animals down into deep, dark mud where there was no oxygen (see Question 15). The animals were rapidly buried without rotting and have therefore been beautifully preserved.

The Burgess Shale animals lived in all kinds of different ways. One group, mainly arthropods, relatives of shrimp, fed in the mud at the bottom of the sea, catching tiny animals as food. Others, largely relatives of snails, swallowed the mud like earthworms do today. Yet another group, mostly early sponges, were filter-feeders: they strained tiny food particles out of the water.

The final group of early animals were carnivores and scavengers. The largest of these was called *Anomalocaris*, a scientific name meaning "strange shrimp." Over 20 in (50 cm) long, it cruised over the bottom mud using rows of rippling flaps along its sides.

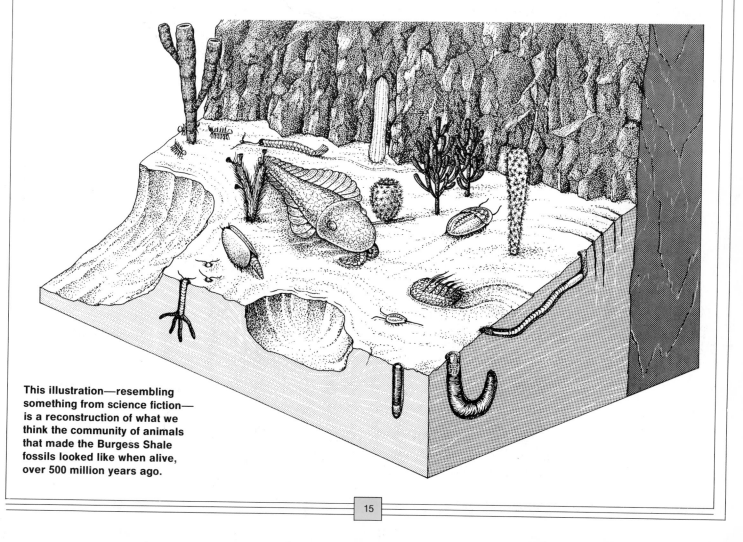

This illustration—resembling something from science fiction—is a reconstruction of what we think the community of animals that made the Burgess Shale fossils looked like when alive, over 500 million years ago.

What is evolution?

Since life began on Earth, the plants and animals that exist on our planet have been changing. Evolution is the word that scientists use to describe these changes through time.

It was one particular scientist, Charles Darwin, who lived from 1809 to 1882, who first worked out how the changes may have happened. Before Darwin, people thought that the world, along with all its creatures, had been made at one point in time, and that nothing had changed since. This idea was still thought to be true even when fossils of long-extinct creatures began to be discovered.

Charles Darwin showed convincingly that creatures do *not* remain the same for all time. His theory of evolution suggested that not only do certain plants and animals die out for ever, but that even while they are alive they are constantly changing. Part of this process of change makes a living thing better suited to its surroundings, which alter through time. Other, more dramatic changes produce entirely new sorts of living things, as shown below. These changes taken together form the process of evolution.

Although Darwin's first ideas have been altered somewhat by more up-to-date knowledge, his basic idea of evolution is still one of the foundations of the modern science of life.

On Darwin's voyage around the world on the *HMS Beagle*, he found different sorts of certain plants and animals that had become adapted for life on different islands in a group called the Galapagos Islands.

Galapagos tortoise

Flightless cormorant

Galapagos land iguana

On an island which had a wet forest zone and a dry desert region, a single species of lizard was found. The lizards had a range of different sorts of claws, including long, hooked ones, straight, pointed ones, and flat, broad ones.

Many thousands of years ago, because of changing weather patterns, the ocean rose and the island was split into two. One of the new islands now has just wet forest vegetation, the other only desert. The lizards are found in both.

The process of evolution happens in the separated island habitats and produces two quite different sorts of lizards. The tree-climbing forest lizard has long, hooked claws for clinging to the trunks. The other, desert lizard burrows in the sand with its flat, broad claws.

13

How does evolution work?

Evolution works because living things are in a continual process of alteration. When animals have young, and new plants grow from seed, the newly formed animals and plants look and behave very much like their parents. But they are never *exactly* the same. The reason for this is that when a male and a female reproduce, the "instructions" for making a new individual —which come half from the father, half from the mother—are shuffled and added to. This shuffling and addition produce the almost endless variety of small differences, any of which can be inherited, or passed on to the next generation.

It is this variety that evolution works on. Some of the slightly different versions of a plant or animal will be a little better at living in particular conditions. Perhaps one can grow faster, another can digest tough grasses more quickly than the others; another might have more resistance to a harmful disease. Most important of all is the fact that any inherited differences that allow the creature to breed better will be passed on more often to the young.

In this way a plant or animal will slowly alter to suit changing environmental conditions. It will, as biologists say, "adapt" to its surroundings in a process that Darwin called "natural selection."

14

Where do new sorts of living things come from?

Every different sort or species of living thing comes from another plant or animal that has lived on this planet. Because distinct species are so different—for instance, cats and dogs—it is usually impossible for them to "blend" together to make a new species.

New species are usually made when animals or plants that once lived together are split apart in some way. The split may be due to a changing landscape—a new desert, a new mountain range, or rising sea levels changing one landmass into two, or into several islands. Because conditions are likely to vary in the separated zones—different weather, or food—this split means that the creatures will gradually change in different ways.

If this "growing apart" of a divided species goes on long enough, it is possible that, if the split populations were to come back into contact again, they would be so different that they would be unable to breed with each other and have young. Two new species will have formed (see below).

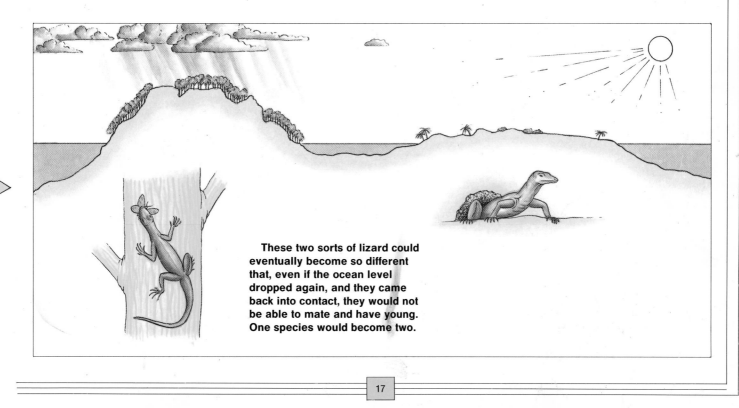

These two sorts of lizard could eventually become so different that, even if the ocean level dropped again, and they came back into contact, they would not be able to mate and have young. One species would become two.

15

How do we know what prehistoric creatures looked like?

Everything we know about what an animal looked like and how it lived when it was crawling around millions of years ago comes from fossils. Fossils are the remains or imprints of long-dead animals, plants, or tiny microbes which have been changed to stone in rocks.

It is usually the strong and resistant "hard parts" of living things that are preserved. This explains why the most common fossils are of bony skeletons, shells, scales, and teeth or the hard mineral parts of animals like corals and sponges. Only if animals are buried very quickly, and with no oxygen (oxygen is needed by the microbes that make soft parts of animals and plants rot away) will there be any chance of other body parts being fossilized.

Some special sorts of fossils give an even more detailed idea of what prehistoric animals looked like. Certain ancient conifers (relations of today's pines and spruces) made a sticky, clear resin when they were cut or damaged. Insects, spiders, and even tree frogs living perhaps 100 million years ago became stuck in this resin, died, and then sank inside it. The resin then hardened and, when the tree trunk was fossilized, the beads of resin turned into fossil lumps of amber with perfectly preserved animals inside them.

16

What is the difference between a stone and a fossil?

There is very little difference between a stone and a fossil. They are both lumps of rock. But the key distinction between them is that the fossil is a rock which has been shaped in the exact form of a living thing that became part of the material from which the rock was made.

Sometimes you can see the fossil standing out very clearly from the surrounding non-fossil rock in which it is embedded. If you look carefully at a chalk cliff face, for instance at the seaside or in a quarry, you may see fossils jutting out of the soft chalk—for example hard sea urchin, sponge, sea-lily stem, and sharks' teeth fossils.

In other cases the fossilized remains are hidden inside balls of rock. Many of the beautiful ammonite fossils are found in such balls, which have to be carefully cracked open with a hammer to show the coiled fossil inside.

17

Can you tell how old a fossil is just by looking at it?

Not really, unless you are a great expert on that particular group of fossils. The fossil expert, or paleontologist, will be able to recognize any ammonite or shark's tooth, for instance, and know from what geological age that species comes.

The rocks in which fossils are found are formed when layer upon layer of mud, lime, or sand slowly builds up on sea-bottoms, in lakes, or deserts. After millions of years, these sediments are turned into solid rock, along with any living things that end up in the sediment layers without decaying.

Usually, the only way to tell the age of a fossil is to know exactly which layer of sedimentary rock it came from. Scientists now know the order in which the rocks were laid down and can therefore find out how old they are. Equally, once we know the ages of certain types of fossils, the mix of fossils that normally occurs in rock of a particular age can be a quick and easy way of dating the rocks.

Fossils from 500-435 million years ago include crinoids (sea lilies) and brachiopods (mollusks).

Even the veins on the wings of this fly, fossilized in amber 30 million years ago, are perfectly preserved.

18

What is a geological age?

To help them study the history of our planet, geologists divide prehistoric time into geological ages. Each age has an identity which depends on the animals and plants alive at that time and now found as fossils. There are often major changes in fossils found at the boundaries between periods, and these geological periods are organized into a type of filing system of rocks and fossils, as shown opposite.

The geological ages are grouped together in even longer time periods called eras. The Precambrian Era comes before all the main fossil-containing rocks were made, and was much longer than any of the succeeding eras.

The word Paleozoic means "early life" and most of the life on Earth at this time was in the seas. The Mesozoic Era, also called the "Age of Dinosaurs," saw the rise and final extinction of these ruling reptiles. In the Cenozoic Era there lived a mixture of animal and plant types similar to those we see around us now on Earth.

The names given to the individual time periods are usually based on the name of the area where fossils of this period were first studied.

19

How long did the ages last?

Each of the geological ages lasted for a different length of time, varying by hundreds of millions of years. This is because their beginnings and endings have been decided on the basis of particular rock types which have been laid down, and the types of fossils which are in them. These boundaries have not, of course, happened at regular intervals, so there would be no sense in having periods that were all the same length. The Cambrian period, for example, lasted for about 85 million years, whereas the later Jurassic period continued for only 35 million years.

The large diagram opposite shows the dates when each of the periods is thought to have begun, and the major groups of animals alive at the time.

PRE-CAMBRIAN ERA

Precambrian Era This era, which lasted nearly 4,000 million years, contains only fossils of the simplest living things like today's bacteria.

PALEOZOIC ERA

Cambrian period During this period all the important groups of animals without backbones arose, and the seas also contained many types of marine algae.

Ordovician period All life was still in the seas: a new group of invertebrate animals called graptolites flourished, and the early jawless fish increased in numbers.

Silurian period Huge sea scorpions were the top marine predators but the first jawed fish also appeared. Plants, scorpions, and millipedes were the first to move from sea onto land.

Devonian period This "Age of Fishes" saw many different types of jawless and jawed fish, including sharks and bony fish. Tree-sized plants and salamanderlike amphibians inhabited swampy forests.

Carboniferous period Many different kinds of animals lived in swamps on land, including spiders, dragonflies, cockroaches, amphibians, and the first reptiles.

Permian period Reptiles took over from amphibians as the major backboned animals on land. In drier, cooler climates, coniferous trees replaced primitive ones.

MESOZOIC ERA

Triassic period Dinosaur reptiles first appeared in this period and some early mammals were also found.

Jurassic period This period saw a great expansion in different types of dinosaurs. Dolphinlike ichthyosaur reptiles were found in the seas. The first birds flew.

Cretaceous period Flowering plants and trees appeared, along with the butterflies and bees that pollinated them. Many plant-eating dinosaurs developed, and massive carnivores like *Tyrannosaurus*.

CENOZOIC ERA

Tertiary period This period saw a great expansion of flowering plants, including grasses, and the formation of vast forests. It was the beginning of the "Age of Mammals."

Quaternary period The last two million years of Earth's history. A severe Ice Age affected the northern hemisphere for much of this period. Humans developed.

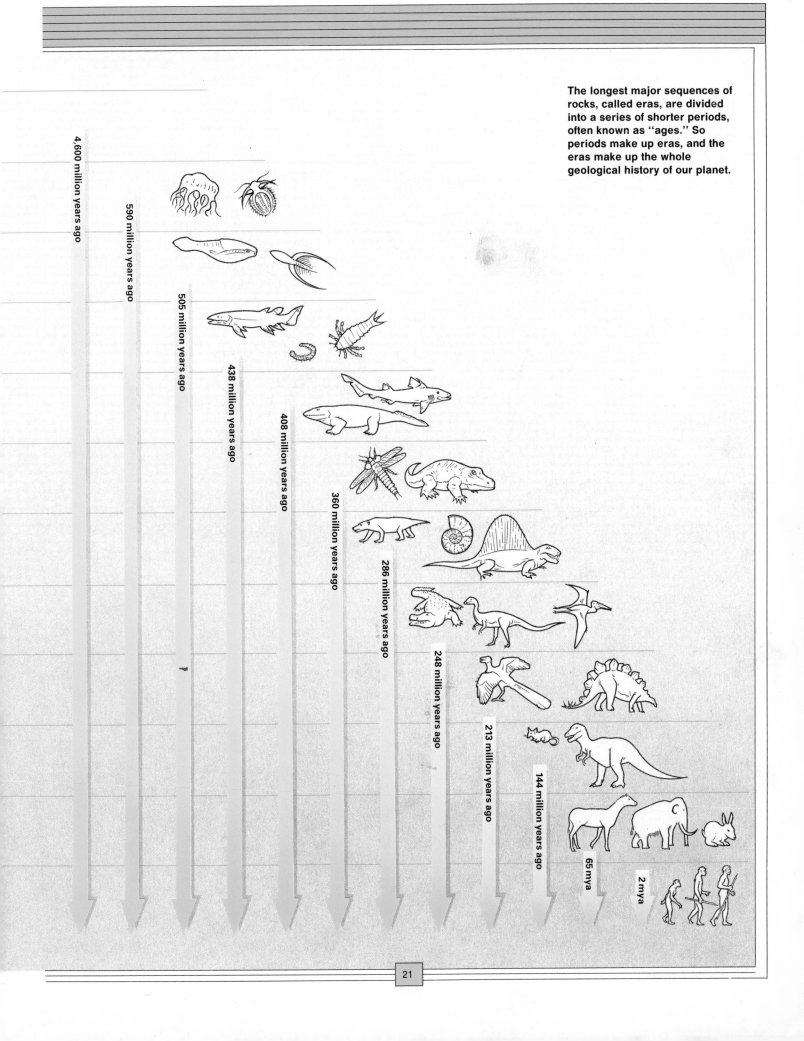

The longest major sequences of rocks, called eras, are divided into a series of shorter periods, often known as "ages." So periods make up eras, and the eras make up the whole geological history of our planet.

4,600 million years ago

590 million years ago

505 million years ago

438 million years ago

408 million years ago

360 million years ago

286 million years ago

248 million years ago

213 million years ago

144 million years ago

65 mya

2 mya

What were the first fish like?

The very first animals to have backbones inside their bodies looked like heavy, armor-plated fish. They did not in fact share all the features of true fish as we know them today—they had no fins and no jaws. For this reason they are known as jawless fish and they first appeared on the Earth over 500 million years ago. Although they evolved in the seas, many forms soon also moved into freshwaters.

Most of these early ancestors of today's fish had bodies covered with thick bony scales and had bony shields over their heads. This "armor" probably gave them some protection from the sea scorpions which were then the largest predators in the seas. Some of these frightening creatures were over 6 ft (2 m) long.

Tiny *Pterapsis* (like most prehistoric creatures, it has no "common" name, only a scientific one) was typical of these early jawless fish. About 8 in (20 cm) long, it had no paired fins and no jaws—just a slit-shaped mouth opening under its pointed head shield. It probably swam in rivers and coastal waters, feeding on tiny crustaceans that formed the plankton of the time. The only jawless fish which still exist today are lampreys and hagfishes which have no armor.

Some 20 to 30 million years later, a variety of fish with jaws and paired fins developed. Over time they provided the ancestors of the three major fish groups that survive today: the sharks and their cousins, which have skeletons made of gristle (cartilage); the common bony fish which have fin rays; and the rarer fleshy-finned fish. *Dipterus* was a 14-in (35-cm) long example of the fleshy-finned type.

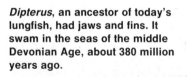

Pterapsis lived in the early Devonian Age, about 400 million years ago. Like other jawless fish, it had heavy "armor plating" covering its head and body.

The prehistoric-looking coelacanth was found in the seas of nearly all the continents of the world 90 million years ago, but its population is now restricted to the Comoro Islands in the western Indian Ocean. There are fears that the continued existence of this living fossil may be endangered by human activities.

Dipterus, an ancestor of today's lungfish, had jaws and fins. It swam in the seas of the middle Devonian Age, about 380 million years ago.

Is there such a thing as a living fossil?

Strictly speaking, of course, there can be no such thing—all fossils are the rocky remains of dead creatures or plants. But there are some animals and plants alive today that are very like those fossilized in the distant past, perhaps hundreds of millions of years ago, and these are often known as living fossils.

The maidenhair tree, or gingko, is a good plant example. It is a type of tree quite separate from all other plants and trees in that it has unique fan-shaped leaves. It is planted in gardens and parks around the world but is native to China. Gingko leaf fossils are known from Jurassic times of about 190 million years ago, when there were many trees of this kind. Now there is only one remaining type, which in its way is a living plant fossil.

Up until the 1930s, coelacanths were a group of fishes known only from 90-million-year-old fossils. But in 1938 a large, living coelacanth was fished out of the water off southern Africa. Suddenly the coelacanth was not a long-extinct form but a living, breathing, breeding fish—a real live fossil.

Coelacanths are still rare. Almost all those found have been fished off the western coast of Grand Comoro Island in the western Indian Ocean. They spend the day in underwater caves some 600 ft (200 m) deep and at night they emerge to hunt other fish. Underwater surveys carried out in 1989 show that there may be only a maximum of 500 coelacanths in the Comoro Islands and two or three of these are fished every year. After 90 million years of survival, the coelacanth now runs the risk of becoming truly extinct.

How did animals get onto the land?

Nobody knows exactly how living things made the great leap forward from being water dwellers to inhabitants of dry land, but the process seems to have begun with plants, then animals without backbones.

For about three billion years before the change, which began about 400 million years ago, all life had been confined to the planet's waters. The land was barren of life. To survive on land, animals had first to be able to avoid drying up once out of water. Second, they had to be able to get the oxygen they needed to breathe direct from air. In addition, they had to develop

ways of breeding which worked in dry land. Not least, their limbs had to eventually be adapted for walking rather than swimming, but that was a later stage.

The earliest land animals we know of from fossils were scorpions and insects, although there might have been other soft-bodied types that were not fossilized.

Only much later, some 350 million years ago, did the first backboned animals move onto land. These were amphibians, which looked rather like fishes on legs. They lived on land but, like today's salamanders and frogs, still returned to the water to breed.

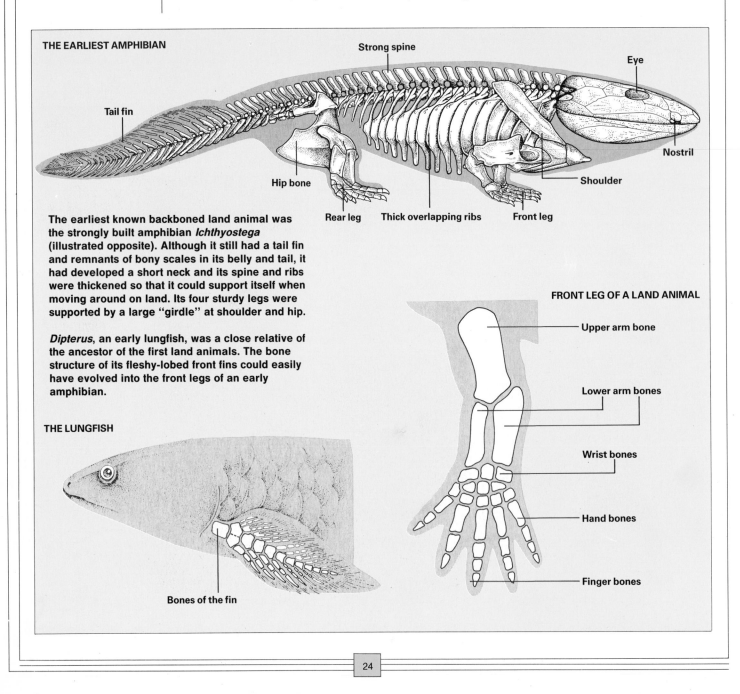

THE EARLIEST AMPHIBIAN

Strong spine · Eye · Tail fin · Nostril · Hip bone · Shoulder · Rear leg · Thick overlapping ribs · Front leg

The earliest known backboned land animal was the strongly built amphibian *Ichthyostega* (illustrated opposite). Although it still had a tail fin and remnants of bony scales in its belly and tail, it had developed a short neck and its spine and ribs were thickened so that it could support itself when moving around on land. Its four sturdy legs were supported by a large "girdle" at shoulder and hip.

Dipterus, an early lungfish, was a close relative of the ancestor of the first land animals. The bone structure of its fleshy-lobed front fins could easily have evolved into the front legs of an early amphibian.

THE LUNGFISH

Bones of the fin

FRONT LEG OF A LAND ANIMAL

Upper arm bone · Lower arm bones · Wrist bones · Hand bones · Finger bones

23

How did the early land animals breathe?

The earliest land vertebrates, the amphibians, breathed air containing the vital gas oxygen in through their mouth and nostrils into lungs. They looked like large, muscular, tough-skinned salamanders but their lungs were even more important to them than they are to today's frogs and salamanders; these creatures have wet, smooth skins through which oxygen can get into the body quickly and directly.

The early amphibians of 350 million years ago had fishlike scales or a tough, dry skin, so they had to take in all the oxygen they needed through their lungs. Like today's salamanders and frogs, the first amphibians also had to lay their eggs in water. These first hatched into tadpoles with gills that took in oxygen from the water. As the young amphibians grew up, the gills were replaced by lungs.

The ancestors of these air-breathing amphibians were probably some of the fleshy-finned fish that swam in the seas and freshwaters of the Late Devonian Age (see Question 20), 390 million years ago. The coelacanth and the lungfish, both fleshy-finned fish, are still alive today, although there are far fewer of them now than there were in those times. Another group of these fish, rhipidistians, were long, streamlined carnivores which looked rather like today's pike. These ancient fish used their fleshy paired fins as short stubby legs and these evolved into the limbs of the early land amphibians. Like their lungfish cousins, the rhipidistians also had lungs of a sort and could breathe air as well as using their gills.

Although no rhipidistian fish still survive today, it is likely that these strange early fish were the ancestors of all types of backboned land animals, including ourselves.

***Ichthyostega* had a fin along its tail and bony scales on its body. Its tail would propel it smoothly along in water, but on land it would have been slow and clumsy.**

***Eryops* was one of the first large amphibians to live on dry land. It was well adapted to walking and feeding on land.**

24

What were the first forests like?

The first forests were dominated by tree-sized fernlike plants that grew to about 100 ft (33 m) high. The first plants to grow on land at all, however, were small and simple and formed meadows, rather than forests. From these, more complex and much larger plants began to develop. During the Devonian Age, about 400 to 360 million years ago, small ferns and then the more massive fernlike trees appeared.

More mixed forests, with plants of many different heights, evolved in the Carboniferous Age, between 350 and 270 million years ago, when the world's weather was warm and damp. The ancient clubmoss *Lepidodendron* and the horsetail *Calamites* reached up to 90 ft (30 m) into the sky. Today plants of these types grow to 3 ft (90 cm) at the most. Other trees included the ancestors of today's gingko tree, monkey puzzles, and cycads.

25

What animals lived in these forests?

The moist forests of the Carboniferous Age were inhabited by a wide range of animals, including fish, amphibians, and even reptiles, as well as many different insects, spiders, and scorpions.

The forests covered much of what is now North America and Europe, which at that time were joined together. The fossils found there tell us that springtail insects jumped among the rotting vegetation, millipedes munched their way through it, and centipedes hunted for worms and other invertebrates, which they paralyzed with their poisoned fangs.

Among the many early insects which flew about between the trees, the most massive were giant dragonflies, with a wingspan of up to 27 in (70 cm)—the jumbo jets of the Carboniferous sky. The amphibians varied in size from those the size and shape of today's salamanders, to enormous, crocodile-sized predators.

In the dense, swampy forests of the Carboniferous Age, giant dragonflies and other insects flew among the towering tree ferns, clubmosses, and horsetails.

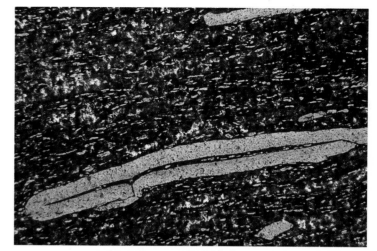

Fragments of a fossilized leaf trapped in coal.

What happened to this forest life when it died?

Many of the plants and animals that died in the Carboniferous forests were eaten by other animals or broken down by the tiny microbes which cause decay. Many others were turned into fossils which have given us a good idea of what the forests looked like and what creatures lived there. A lot of the fossilized, often partly rotted, plant material built up as peat. This eventually turned into coal. The name of this geological age—the Carboniferous—in fact means "coal bearing."

Dead plants that fell into the swamp's mud were often buried before they could decay significantly. Much of this mud had so little oxygen in it that microbes were virtually unable to decompose the plants and tree trunks.

Over many thousands and then millions of years, thick layers of this preserved plant material built up as peat, which was later covered by layers of mud. When this mud was pressed down by the weight of the layers above it and slowly turned into rock, the plant material itself slowly altered and, in the end, turned into the black substance we call coal.

Can plants become fossils?

Almost any living thing can be turned into a fossil provided the conditions are right. When it dies, it must be trapped in mud or sediment in a way which preserves some of its body structure while the sediments are slowly turning into rock.

Plants are no exception to this rule. Almost any sort of plant—from minute, single-celled algae to giant forest trees—may form a fossil. As with animals, it is always the hard, resistant parts of plants that turn into fossils most easily; soft parts which rot quickly only rarely make fossils. This explains why there are many places around the world where fossilized wood may be found, but very few examples of fossil flowers.

We have fossils of some of the earliest and simplest green plants, including single-celled algae and other seaweeds that lived in the seas of prehistory. Even the tiniest plants played a vital role in the formation of certain sedimentary rocks. Some of the structure of chalk, for instance, is made up of the microscopic fossilized limey plates (each less than 0.01 mm across) that surrounded the cells of sea-dwelling algae in the Cretaceous Age.

Larger land plants have made many different types of fossil. Fossils of parts of 90-ft (30-m) high clubmosses of the Carboniferous Age, for instance, have formed from the bark, trunks, and branches with leaves and cones, as well as their branched, anchoring rootlike structures.

A Carboniferous Age fossil fern, 360-290 million years old, buried in coal.

The Petrified Forest in Arizona's National Park.

How are trees fossilized?

Trees that have been turned to coal or to stone are sometimes fossilized in their natural growing position—with the roots at the base and all the trunks pointing upward. In other cases the fossil tree trunks are jumbled up in a way which suggests that they were fossilized after they had fallen together and floated in a great mass along rivers and into lakes. This is known as a logjam.

A fossil forest is a place where large numbers of fossilized tree trunks lie on the ground close together, near to where they once grew. They may be found anywhere where softer surrounding rocks have been worn away to reveal the tougher tree fossils beneath. Fossil forests are most commonly seen on a seashore, where waves have caused the erosion, or in deserts, where wind-blown sand has been the rock-wearing force.

Fossil forests can be found all over the world and have been formed from trees of many different periods. Famous fossil forests are known on the Greek island of Lesbos and in the Painted Desert of northeastern Arizona in the United States. The Arizona desert petrified forest was formed from trees that grew in the Triassic Age about 200 million years ago. At that time, ancient relatives of modern monkey-puzzlelike trees grew tall on the flood plains of wide rivers flowing through a landscape where there were many active volcanoes.

Millions of tree trunks were sometimes buried all at once when volcanoes erupted. When Mount St. Helens, a volcano in western Canada, erupted in 1980, it flattened many millions of trees that grew close to the mountain. Some lakes in the area were filled from end to end with the dead, blasted trunks. Many trees were also buried upright, *in situ*. The same type of catastrophe happened several times in the ancient past. The illustrations on the right show one sequence of events that might have created a fossil logjam.

THE CREATION OF A FOSSIL LOGJAM

1. Many millions of years ago, tall pines and other trees grew on a vast flood plain, in a region active with volcanoes.

2. When the trees died, from whatever cause, some were washed by floods into the rivers, and made logjams at river bends and in lakes. Many also remained upright and were buried in their original positions after a volcanic eruption.

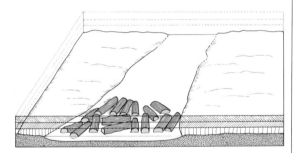

3. Once the logjam became covered by layers of mud, silt, and volcanic ash, its fossilization had begun. Minerals including silica seeped into the dead wood from the surrounding sediments, which finally turned the trunks into beautiful crystalline replicas of the originals.

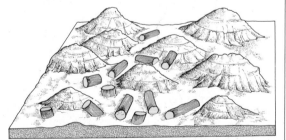

4. The sediments around them turned into softer shales and sandstones. When, millions of years later, the softer sediments were eroded away, the petrified remains of the original trunks lay exposed—a reminder of the forest that had stood there hundreds of millions of years before.

29

Were all dinosaurs big and fierce?

Dinosaurs—the "terrible lizards"—were by no means all big and fierce. While some dinosaurs were as tall as a three-story building or as heavy as a 30-ton whale, others were only the size of a chicken. And although certain dinosaurs had sharp claws and vicious teeth for tearing apart the flesh of their prey, others were peaceful plant-eaters and grazed quietly in herds or browsed among the treetops.

Tyrannosaurus rex, one of the best known of all the dinosaurs, was certainly big and fierce, however. This giant predator, whose name means "tyrant lizard," lived about 70 million years ago in the Late Cretaceous Age, toward the end of the dinosaur era. It stood nearly 18 ft (6 m) tall and was about 48 ft (15 m) from head to tail. Its mouth was filled with huge fangs, each about 6 in (15 cm) long, and its hind legs had vicious claws on the toes.

T. rex is the most fiercesome example of one type of meat-eating dinosaur, the carnosaurs, which were all big and powerful and walked on two legs. But the other meat-eaters, the coelurosaurs, were lightly built, fast-running dinosaurs, which fed on small prey, such as mammals, lizards, and insects.

The illustrations on this page show three out of the many different types of dinosaur that existed.

30

What color were dinosaurs?

No one knows. The color of an animal's skin is one of the first things to be lost after it dies, even if, in time, it turns into a fossil. The chemicals that make up some of the colors fade and then rot away soon after the animal has stopped living.

Even when the tough skin of a dinosaur has been preserved as a fossil, it does not show any of the colors or markings that it would have had when alive. Its color will be that of the mineral in the fossil rock.

When they create illustrations of dinosaurs, scientists and artists have to guess what colors and patterns to choose. These guesses are based partly on the range of colors and patterns seen in today's reptiles and partly on what we know about the way of life and habitats of the different dinosaurs.

Oviraptor, up to 6 ft (2 m) long, had beaklike jaws with no teeth and ate the eggs of other dinosaurs.

Hypsilophodon, 6ft (2 m) long, was the gazelle of the dinosaur world. Many of these fast-running plant-eating dinosaurs lived together in herds.

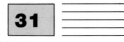

31

Were dinosaurs warm-blooded?

For many years biologists who studied the fossilized remains of dinosaurs thought that these animals must all have been cold-blooded, like today's reptiles and amphibians. That is to say, they would have had the same temperature as the air around them, whatever the weather; they would have been unable to control their temperature and keep it high like warm-blooded birds and mammals do today.

Some fossil experts have suggested that certain of the larger dinosaurs might have been warm-blooded. But keeping a constant body temperature uses up a lot of food. It is difficult to see how some of the huge plant-eating dinosaurs could have eaten enough to provide the energy to keep their vast bodies at a high temperature, especially since they lacked good insulation like hair or feathers.

Some large dinosaurs may have kept a high body temperature partly by making energy from their food and partly by their lifestyle, for instance moving in and out of the Sun to keep them warm. Another idea is that the large plates on the backs of dinosaurs like *Stegosaurus* could have been thermal panels, picking up solar heat when face on to the Sun. We will probably never know the whole truth.

Tyrannosaurus rex was the terror of the dinosaur world. It had a huge body, weighing more than an elephant, and its massive head was filled with big, razor-sharp teeth shaped like steak knives, with serrations down the side. Its powerful jaws would have been big enough to swallow a person whole.

What was the "Age of the Dinosaurs?"

In the Age of the Dinosaurs, which began some 205 million years ago, the dinosaurs and other ancient reptiles roamed the Earth. These amazing creatures continued to rule the planet until they mysteriously died out 65 million years ago. During this time the world saw many changes: continents moved, sea levels altered, climates changed, and many new creatures and plants appeared as well as others becoming extinct.

While the dinosaurs of many sorts and sizes were masters of the land, the flying pterosaurs (including the well-known pterodactyls) held sway in the skies as gliders and fliers; and the crocodiles—with their powerful armored bodies, sturdy limbs, and swimming tails—dominated pools, lakes, rivers, and swamps.

When the dinosaurs disappeared they had existed for more than 140 million years. In contrast, mammals have been the dominant land animals only for the 65 million years since then. People have only walked on the planet for between four and two million years. So the mammals have got another 75 million years to go before they catch up with the dinosaurs!

Euparkeria was an early land-dwelling reptile that lived in the rocks of southern Africa during the Triassic Age, about 240 million years ago. Its powerful hind limbs were a third longer than the front ones and, while it probably spent most of its time moving on all fours, it would have reared up on its back legs for bursts of speed.

Were the dinosaurs reptiles?

Yes, they certainly were. In fact they were the most successful group of reptiles that ever lived. They had skeletons like those of reptiles, and the same scaly skin but they had other features that made them special.

Some of the dinosaurs' ancestors had already made a change to a rapid and flexible method of walking and running. Their earliest ancestors held their bodies flat on the ground, with the knees and elbow joints stuck out sideways, but later the knees and elbows were shifted underneath the body so that the trunk was lifted off the ground and the weight of the body was supported on straight legs. Some creatures also became able to run on their toes rather than on their feet.

The dinosaurs took this development a stage further and many of them became two-legged. Walking on their hind legs freed their arms for other important jobs, such as catching prey.

A typical reptile moves with a sprawling motion since its legs are splayed out to the sides. Its whole body twists from side to side at each step, as shown by the line of its backbone and its hip and shoulder "girdles".

How many sorts of dinosaurs were there?

Probably there were over 400, from gigantic creatures plodding along on all fours down to agile, fast-running birdlike sorts. There were meat-eating carnivores, plant-eating herbivores, and omnivores, not fussy in their feeding habits.

Scientists divide the dinosaurs into two main groups—the lizard-hipped and the bird-hipped dinosaurs—according to the design of their skeletons. As the name suggests, the most important differences have to do with the design of the hips, and the way the hip bones have been changed for walking on the hind legs only.

The lizard-hipped types of dinosaur did not in fact all walk on two legs. In general, the meat-eaters did while the plant-eaters supported their heavy bodies on four stout limbs. *Tyrannosaurus* was a two-legged lizard-hipped carnivore, while the even more massive *Brachiosaurus* and *Diplodocus* were typical lizard-hipped herbivores. All the bird-hipped dinosaurs were herbivores, with jaws beautifully adapted for eating plants.

Lesothaurus was a plant-eating bird-hipped dinosaur. Its light build, long legs, and short arms enabled it to run at speed.

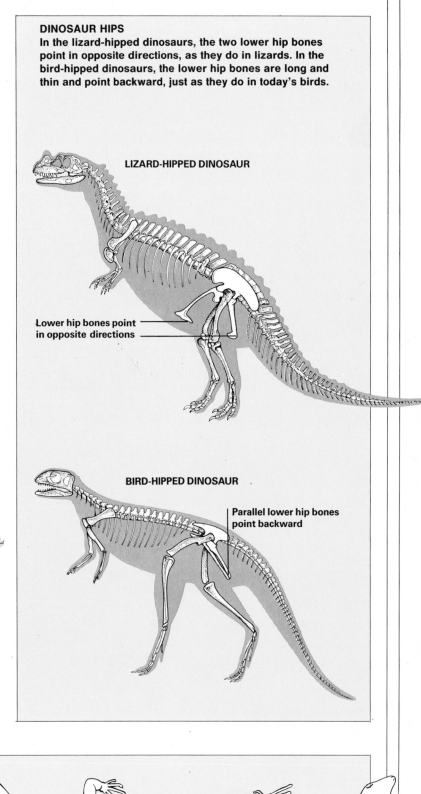

DINOSAUR HIPS
In the lizard-hipped dinosaurs, the two lower hip bones point in opposite directions, as they do in lizards. In the bird-hipped dinosaurs, the lower hip bones are long and thin and point backward, just as they do in today's birds.

LIZARD-HIPPED DINOSAUR

Lower hip bones point in opposite directions

BIRD-HIPPED DINOSAUR

Parallel lower hip bones point backward

What was a pterodactyl?

The pterodactyls were a sophisticated group of prehistoric flying and gliding reptiles related to the crocodiles and the dinosaurs. This group of winged reptiles is called the pterosaurs or "winged lizards."

These prehistoric fliers first lived in the late Triassic Age, over 200 million years ago—and 50 million years before the first known bird. They had skin-covered wings, which stretched between one enormously long "finger" on each hand and the back legs, and were attached to the sides of the body. The remaining "fingers" of each hand were short claws at the front edge of the wing. The early pterosaurs had long tails and jaws with teeth.

The later pterodactyls had toothless jaws and very short tails. They were probably poor fliers but accomplished gliders; many of them seem to have soared high above the ground on rising thermals (warm currents of air).

Among the pterodactyls was *Quetzalocoatlus*, the largest animal ever to fly. With a wingspan of 40 ft (12 m), it was wider than a house and weighed nearly 150 lb (68 kg). Its long neck and toothless, pointed jaws would have enabled it to probe inside the carcass of a rotting dinosaur.

Were there birds in the sky when the dinosaurs lived?

Yes, there were. The earliest true birds were warm-blooded backboned animals, quite different from the winged lizards because they had feathers. They evolved from small, meat-eating dinosaurs and shared the world with the dinosaurs, flying in the same skies as the pterosaurs. However, when the last of the flying reptiles became extinct at the end of the Cretaceous Age, the feathered birds carried on, and there are about 9,000 kinds in the world today.

Nearly everything we know about the earliest birds comes from some detailed and beautiful fossils dating from about 150 million years ago. They are of the first bird we know, called *Archaeopteryx*. It was about 15 in (38 cm) long, and around the size of a pigeon. Although it was like a reptile in many ways—it had sharp, pointed teeth in its jaws, claws on its wings, and a long, bony tail—it was undoubtedly a bird that flew, because the fossils show both wings and feathers.

Although *Archaeopteryx* had a wishbone like modern birds, it did not have their huge breastbone onto which the flight muscles ("breast meat") are attached. This suggests that *Archaeopteryx* was not a strong flier.

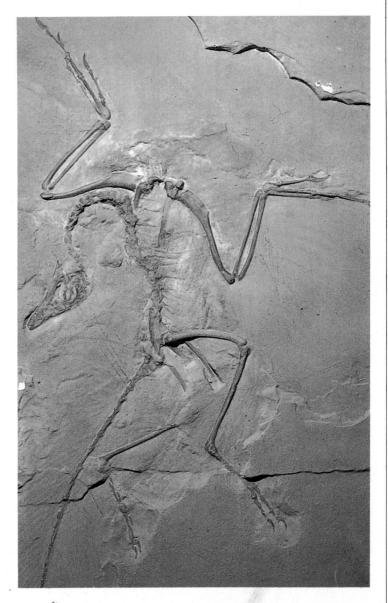

The fossilized remains of *Archaeopteryx* (above), the first known bird, were discovered in southern Germany in the 1930s. Because they were preserved in fine-grained sediments, we can clearly make out the feathers of the wings and tail, its twisted head and neck, and the claws on its wings.

A reconstruction of *Archaeopteryx* (left) shows its large wings, long legs, and boned tail. Scientists think it may have used its clawed wings and feet to climb trees, before gliding or flapping from one tree to another.

37

Has any human ever seen a living dinosaur?

Unfortunately the answer to this intriguing question is no. By the time that people first walked on the face of the Earth, the last dinosaur had been extinct for a very long time—over 60 million years. So neither our own species nor our close ape ancestors has ever come into contact with a living dinosaur.

All our pictures of dinosaurs, the names we give to them, and the wonderful moving, full-size models that you can now see in some museums, are re-creations based on the fossilized remains found in rocks around the world. Using this information, we have had to reconstruct what we think these awe-inspiring animals looked like.

The exciting films and television programs that show modern explorers or primitive cavemen battling bravely with ferocious dinosaurs, or being attacked from the skies by dive-bombing pterodactyls, are in no way based on prehistoric fact. While the group-hunting methods of those early people might well have enabled them to trap a dinosaur for food, people came onto the landscape 60 million years too late to try them out. Nevertheless, these fanciful battles make thrilling movies!

38

Where are dinosaurs found?

Fossil hunters are still finding new types of dinosaurs in sedimentary rocks all over the world formed in Triassic, Jurassic, and Cretaceous times (see page 21).

The first fossilized dinosaur bones and teeth were collected in the early nineteenth century. They came from the rocks of southern England and were given their first scientific names in 1824 and 1825. But it was not until 1841 that Sir Richard Owen, who later became Director of the British Museum (Natural History), realized that these strange and gigantic animals like *Iguanodon* belonged to a completely separate and so far undiscovered group of reptiles. He gave the name dinosaur—(meaning "terrible lizard")—to these long-extinct animals.

When the dinosaurs first came into the world at the end of the Triassic Age, some 205 million years ago, all the landmasses of the planet were connected together in a super-continent called Pangea. This meant that the early dinosaurs could roam to all regions of the world without having to cross seas.

Throughout the Jurassic Age and until the later part of the Cretaceous Age, all types of dinosaurs were found throughout the world. Once Pangea began to break up, and with the opening of the Atlantic Ocean to the west of Africa, fossils show that different types of dinosaurs developed in particular parts of the world. The greatest number of different dinosaur types has been found in North America, in Europe, and in Asia.

Can new dinosaurs still be found today?

Yes, completely new groups of dinosaurs are still being discovered.

One of the most recent finds is a new family of meat-eating (carnivorous) dinosaurs from the early part of the Cretaceous Age. The only member of this family found so far was discovered by an amateur fossil hunter in a brick-clay pit in southern England in 1983. It has been scientifically named *Baryonyx walkeri*, after Mr Walker who discovered it, but it has the more catchy nickname of "Claws."

Claws was a 26–32 ft (8–10 m) long carnivore with a crocodile-shaped head filled with many sharp, pointed teeth. It probably walked on either two or four legs and on each of its forefeet one toe was enlarged to form a huge curved claw about 12 in (30 cm) long.

In the region where the creature's intestines would have been, the *Baryonyx* fossil contained scales and teeth of a large, lagoon-living fish. Scientists think that this dinosaur lived close to the water's edge and got its meals rather like grizzly bears do today, by hooking fish out of the water with its claws.

THE STORY OF "CLAWS"
The astonishing size and curved shape of the large claw found next to the skeleton of *Baryonyx* earned this newly discovered dinosaur its nickname of "Claws." The 12-in (30-cm) long claw is shown below next to *Baryonyx's* normal finger and in scale with an adult human's hand, to illustrate its size.

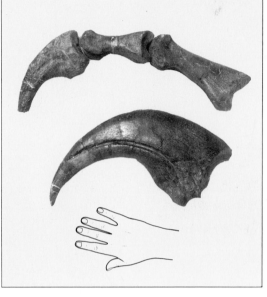

Scientists think that *Baryonyx* hunted along the banks of rivers and lakes, using its large claws like a harpoon, to hook fish out of the water.

Why did the dinosaurs die out?

Scientists are not really sure what made the last of the species of dinosaurs die out at the end of the Cretaceous Age. But they have several interesting theories about what might have happened 65 million years ago.

One exciting recent idea is that the Earth at that time suffered a collision with a huge asteroid or meteorite. A big enough object falling to Earth from space would have produced an explosive force and damage similar to that of an all-out nuclear war. Vast amounts of dust, steam, and smoke pushed into the atmosphere would block out the Sun's heat and light for a very long time. This lack of light could well have killed off many land plants, and therefore caused the deaths of both the plant-eating dinosaurs and the carnivorous dinosaurs that fed on them. If the climate cooled down a lot, due to the dust in the atmosphere, this could also have contributed to the extinction of dinosaurs adapted for warm conditions.

There seems to be some good evidence for this "space invader" explanation of the end of the dinosaurs. In the rocks formed 65 million years ago there is a thin band containing metals like osmium and iridium that are rare in ordinary Earth rocks but commoner in some types of meteorite. Perhaps the metals arrived from space. The band also contains tiny shattered particles of glass, made from fused sand grains, like those formed in intense explosions, and fossilized soot particles which may have come from forest fires caused by the fireball of a large meteorite impact.

We do not know for sure if this is the correct explanation for the loss of the dinosaurs. Similar effects on the climate might have been produced by greatly increased volcanic activity.

Both *Corythosaurus* (right), a duckbilled dinosaur, and *Ankylosaurus* (below, right), the largest-known armored dinosaur, survived right up to the end of the Cretaceous Age.

The flying reptiles (*Pteranodon*, left) and the long-necked marine reptiles (like *Elasmosaurus*, right) also died out when the dinosaurs did.

41

Did other creatures die out at the same time?

Yes they did. When talking of the extinction of the dinosaurs, it is easy to forget that on the land and in the sea many other large groups of creatures were dying out at the same time. The fact that both marine and land animals all suffered together suggests that the cause must have been large enough to affect both the oceans and dry land equally.

On land, the fabulous flying and gliding reptiles called pterosaurs, the "winged lizards", (see Question 35) disappeared at almost exactly the same time as their

dinosaur cousins. In the seas and oceans, the swimming reptiles with long necks and four limb paddles, called plesiosaurs, became extinct. So, too, did the belemnites and ammonites—two ancient groups of relatives of octopus and squid. Even microscopic planktonic organisms lost many species.

This disappearance of such a wide range of types of animals at one time is called a "mass extinction." The mass extinction at the end of the Cretaceous Age set the scene for the development and evolution of a modern mixture of animal types. The major groups of animals that survived the mass extinction 65 million years ago were the direct ancestors of today's familiar animals. We can see them all around us today—mammals, birds, lizards, crocodiles, turtles, fish, snails, and shellfish. Their ancestors drew the lucky numbers in the lottery 65 million years ago. The animals that drew unlucky numbers left no descendants: you see no descendants today of the dinosaurs or the ammonites.

Where did the first mammals come from?

The ancestors of the mammals, which are the world's most successful modern group of animals, were ancient reptiles.

The great difference between mammals and reptiles is that they are warm-blooded—that is, they can keep their bodies warm all the time. Instead of depending on the Sun to warm them up, mammals eat large amounts of food and burn it up quickly to turn it into heat.

This new method of controlling their body temperature by eating more food required better jaws and teeth, and a more efficient way of walking. The mammals also needed better insulation to hold heat in their bodies. The chief way in which mammals conserve heat is by their covering of hair.

Another distinguishing mark of a mammal is the one which gives the group its name—female mammals have breasts (mammary glands), which produce nutritious milk to feed the young until they can find food for themselves.

The earliest mammal ancestors, a group of "mammal-like reptiles" called pelycosaurs, have all died out, so are known only from fossils. These creatures roamed the Earth in the late Carboniferous Age. Some pelycosaurs could control their body temperature by means of heat-regulating "sails" on their backs. The sail allowed the creature to absorb heat from the Sun, or to cool down, as it needed.

The therapsids, which appeared in the Triassic Age, were the direct ancestors of mammals. Only one group, the cynodonts, survived into the Jurassic Age. Fossils of these mammal-like reptiles date from about 220–190 million years ago.

HOW THE SKULL CHANGED
The opening behind the eye socket became larger, to allow for longer jaw muscles, until the eye socket and opening merged. The lower jaw enlarged and became one bone instead of several.

THE BODY OF A MAMMAL ANCESTOR
Thrinaxodon, illustrated on the facing page, had many of the features of early mammals. It walked like a mammal, with its legs beneath its body, and one of its foot bones had developed a heel. It had strong teeth and powerful jaws for biting. Its long body was divided into a chest and lower back region, the division marked by the extent of the ribs. The rib cage would have protected its heart and lungs.

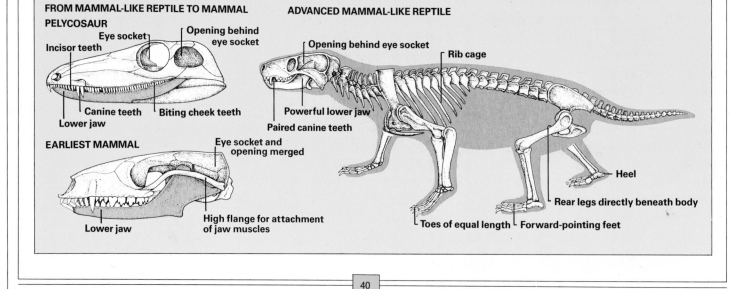

FROM MAMMAL-LIKE REPTILE TO MAMMAL

PELYCOSAUR

Eye socket

Opening behind eye socket

Incisor teeth

Canine teeth

Biting cheek teeth

Lower jaw

EARLIEST MAMMAL

Eye socket and opening merged

High flange for attachment of jaw muscles

Lower jaw

ADVANCED MAMMAL-LIKE REPTILE

Opening behind eye socket

Rib cage

Powerful lower jaw

Paired canine teeth

Heel

Rear legs directly beneath body

Toes of equal length

Forward-pointing feet

Thrinaxodon

Cynognathus **(left) was a cynodont, one of the group of powerful mammal-like reptiles that walked like mammals, with their elbows and knees under their body. Scientists think it was covered in hair since the bones of the animal's snout had tiny holes called "whisker pits," resembling those found under the big whiskers of modern cats.**

A swimming platypus searches the bottom of the water for insect larvae.

Did the early mammals lay eggs?

At least one group of primitive mammals almost certainly laid eggs, like their reptile ancestors did. This egg-laying group were the ancient relatives of the modern mammals called monotremes, which includes the echidnas (spiny anteaters) and duckbilled platypus, found in Australia.

These mammals have fur and milk-making mammary glands, but, unlike all other modern groups of mammals, they also lay eggs. The ancestors of today's monotremes were small animals ranging in size from that of a shrew to a squirrel. They were either predators, hunting insects, tiny animals, and small reptiles, or they were plant-eaters with teeth that were designed for grinding up tough vegetation, as rats and other rodents do today. They lived in a world that was ruled by the dinosaurs.

One reason for our uncertainty about these early groups is the lack of conclusive evidence: the tiny, soft-shelled eggs that such creatures would have laid would rarely have been fossilized.

The other reason is that we do not yet know enough about the way the various groups of early mammals developed from one another. It is not certain whether all groups of modern mammals evolved from the same ancient creatures as the monotremes, or whether the mammals that do not lay eggs came from quite a different set of prehistoric mammal ancestors which had already given up egg laying.

44

Who became the top beasts after the dinosaurs?

When the last of the dinosaurs died out 65 million years ago, the warm-blooded mammals became the dominant large land animals and have remained so ever since.

Early mammals in fact lived on Earth throughout the time that dinosaurs were around. But the mammals alive then were an unimportant group of small animals, no bigger than rats. While the dinosaurs ruled the Earth, they stopped the mammals diversifying. But mammals did manage to survive whatever it was—catastrophic falling meteorite or dramatic change of climate—that caused the mass extinction at the end of the Cretaceous Age.

Perhaps with their high body temperatures (being warm-blooded), they were able to feed and be active at night. Being small, the mammals could hide underground or in rock crevices to avoid being caught and eaten during the day.

With their competitors gone, the mammals started to develop along different routes, and to become bigger and more complex. Only after the dinosaurs died out did true mammals exceed the size of small dogs. But many new groups of specialist mammals then evolved, and they fell into two main groups: the marsupials, in which the babies developed for a while in a pouch, and the placentals, in which the young grew to an advanced stage in the mother's womb. Most mammals today, including humans, are the placental type.

45

Where did horses come from?

Horses are one of the evolutionary success stories among the plant-eating hoofed mammals known as ungulates. From the time of the extinction of the dinosaurs onward, the basic body plan for the placental mammals has been turned into animals as different as shrews, mice, hedgehogs, monkeys, bats, whales, seals, dogs, bears, cats, elephants, cows, and horses. Luckily, scientists have an excellent detailed fossil record for the horse group.

Hoofed mammals can be sorted into several natural groupings. One—to which horses, rhinoceroses, and tapirs belong—is the "odd-toed" ungulates since their feet usually have an odd number of toes. Horses themselves gradually reduced their number of toes, finally retaining only the middle one.

Horses began as cat-sized animals that browsed on forest plants about 55 million years ago. As they evolved, their number of toes reduced, and their stance became more erect; both changes improved their running speed. At the same time the animals grew much larger in size, their neck became longer, and their jaws and teeth were improved for chewing tough grass food efficiently. All these changes allowed them to make the best use of grassland, to which horses are now well adapted.

How did the giraffe get its long neck?

The giraffe got its long neck by a gradual development from ancestors that had much shorter necks, but whose mouths cropped tough vegetation just like today's giraffes do. The giraffe's ancestors, because they found themselves in competition with many other plant-eaters for the vegetation in the bushlands they inhabited, became specialized for cropping the leaves from trees at a great height—higher than could be reached by any of their competitor species. This evolutionary track produced an animal with very long legs and an exceptionally long neck.

The giraffes and their relatives belong to the group of hooved mammals that have an even number of toes on their feet. This collection of herbivorous mammals includes pigs, hippopotamus, camels, cows, sheep, deer, and antelopes as well as the giraffes.

The even-toed group first appeared over 50 million years ago and in the end became the most successful group of large plant-eating land mammals. This success was mainly due to their complicated gut which was able to cope with digesting tough plant material very efficiently. It does this with the help of the stomach's "fermentation chambers" which contain microbes that break down the food into substances that the animal can use.

Prolibytherium was a small, early relative of antelopes, deer, and giraffe. it had two flattened hornlike structures on its head, which may have been skin-covered in life.

47 Is evolution still going on?

Yes, as long as there are living plants, animals, and microbes on the Earth, the slow but steady process of evolution will continue (see Question 12). Over periods of time that can be measured in thousands or even millions of years, living things will become continually better able to deal with their changing environment. At the same time, new sorts of animals and plants will evolve from those that have existed before.

While the process of evolution makes new types of living things, at the same time other sorts are disappearing as they become extinct. In the addition sum of nature, the total number of species of living things usually stays about the same: gains are balanced by losses.

It is difficult for scientists to predict what major changes await us in the future. Whereas in the past animals changed to fit their surroundings better, humans are now able to change their surroundings to fit their needs—for example, by growing crops and building houses. It seems likely that the ways in which human beings have changed their world will have a great impact on future evolution.

Gigantopithecus was an awesome ape standing some 10 ft (3 m) tall.

48 Is the yeti a prehistoric animal?

Although it has not yet been described properly by scientists, the yeti is said to be a giant apelike creature living in the snows of the high, inaccessible peaks of the Himalayan mountain range. Another creature which has the same kind of mysterious reputation is the "Bigfoot" in North America.

Most scientists do not believe in these animals. They feel that, with modern methods of investigation, it would be almost impossible for such large animals to survive and breed without leaving traces of themselves—dead carcasses or bones, for instance. The only evidence for the yeti to date is photographs of rather melted footprints in the snow and some fur which most scientists think is monkey fur.

One theory which has been considered is that the yeti might be a surviving mountain population of a gigantic fossil gorilla called *Gigantopithecus*, which really did live in Asia between four and one million years ago. Fossils of its jaws and teeth from rocks of that period have been discovered. But most serious scientists will not accept this theory of the yeti without more supporting evidence.

Muraenosaurus, whose real fossilized remains date from 160 million years ago.

Could the Loch Ness monster be a living fossil?

The blurred outline of the Loch Ness "monster," photographed in 1961.

Some people believe that the Loch Ness monster, perhaps the most famous mystery animal in the world, is a living fossil—an ancient aquatic reptile like *Muraenosaurus*, above. But it has to be said that most scientists dispute this.

Loch Ness is a deep lake in Scotland, in whose waters there have been many supposed sightings of a gigantic water creature. Most stories about the monster rely on photographs taken at the loch which reveal blurred shapes in the water. Some of these shapes could be taken for a long curved neck with a small head sticking out of the water. Others show a series of raised humps in the murky waters of the loch.

One serious problem with the living fossil theory is that there have been no fossilized remains found for the last 65 million years or so. Another is that an animal like this would be easily traced with modern sonar techniques which are sensitive enough to pick up single fish. No sonar surveys of Loch Ness have detected echoes from large unidentified objects.

Finally, for there to be so many sightings, there would have to be several families of the animals in the Loch. But no bones, teeth, or other remains of dead monsters have even been found. For these reasons, most scientists think of the Loch Ness monster in the same way as fantasy animals like unicorns and dragons.

We should always have a small doubt in our minds, though, before saying that such creatures could *never* exist. At the beginning of this century no scientist had ever seen an okapi, a relative of the giraffe: it was only discovered in 1911. Also at that time, no sensible scientist would have given any odds on there being live coelacanths in the sea (see Question 21), yet in 1938 a fisherman pulled just such a living fossil fish out of the waters off southern Africa. These examples should teach us that evolution and animal survival are complicated processes which can still provide us with great surprises.

Did our species really evolve from apes?

Yes, it did. Just as mammals and birds arose from reptiles that existed before them, and amphibians evolved from fish, we too arose from creatures that lived on Earth before us.

If we look around us in the animal kingdom for clues about who our ancestors might have been, the answers about our origins become obvious. There are very few other mammals apart from ourselves that can walk on two legs, have no tail to speak of, have faces without a long snout, have eyes on the front of the head that look straight ahead, and that possess big brains. Apart from ourselves, only the apes have all these characteristics.

Scientists are now able to examine the genes of different animals—the inherited material that makes each animal what it is—and compare the genes of one animal with those of another. When the genes of people and chimpanzees are compared, it turns out that almost all the human genes are identical with those of the chimp. This proves beyond doubt that we are closely related to apes. Our closest living relatives among other animals are gorillas, chimpanzees, and orang utans: we and these living apes must have evolved from earlier forms of ape.

What is so special about being human?

Although humans are apes, we are unusual and very accomplished ones. We differ from other apes in several ways. First of all, we are less hairy and our bodies are specialized for walking upright on two legs all the time. Our hands have fingers and thumbs that, used together, are much more flexible and better able to grasp small objects than those of other apes.

Our more important special features

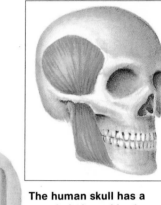

The human skull has a rounded, domed braincase to enclose its large brain. The face is flat with only slight eyebrow ridges. The teeth are even in size and the jaw muscles are of moderate size.

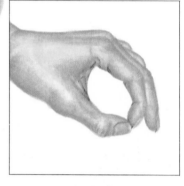

The human hand has long, mobile fingers and a long thumb. The thumb may be moved around on its base so it can be brought up to all the other fingertips. This means that small objects can be held with great control.

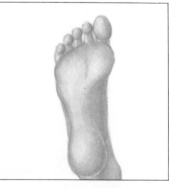

The human foot is designed entirely for walking on two legs. The toes are short and they all point forward. The big toe is in line with the other toes.

The human skeleton

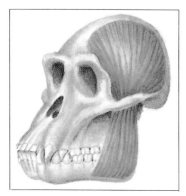

The gorilla's skull holds a much smaller brain; it has a pointed snout area and large "eyebrow ridges." The jaw-closing muscles are attached to the large top ridge. The large teeth are uneven in size and include canines.

The gorilla's hand has long fingers but a much shorter thumb. This difference in the lengths and in the organization of the joints means that the thumbtip cannot be brought together with the fingertips.

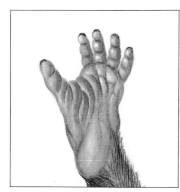

The gorilla's foot is designed both for walking and for gripping onto branches. The toes are longer than in humans and the big toes point sideways.

have less to do with how our bodies are made than with what we can do. This is due to our greater intelligence, a result of having developed much bigger brains than apes. Because of our greater brain power, we humans have speech. We use our language to communicate with other members of our species. Although many apes can use tools, we have developed this ability much further. It has enabled us to build homes, make weapons, cook food and, over the thousands of years since humans evolved, to create great civilizations.

The gorilla's skeleton

Can you find fossils of early humans?

Yes, you can. Early humans—that is, early members of our species and those of more apelike humans with whom we share distant relatives—have left fossils just as other long-dead animals have done. Unfortunately, there are very few complete ones (see Question 53).

The fossils of ancient humans are nearly all of human bones or teeth; they were formed when their bodies became embedded in different types of mud and sediments (see Question 16). Some are in sedimentary rocks that formed in caves, some in rocks made by lake sediments, and others are buried in layers made from the ash and debris from volcanoes which erupted long ago.

As well as bones, we can also find objects made by those ancient peoples, such as stone knives, weapons, pots, and buildings. There are even footprints planted in soft mud. These became fossil footprints when the mud eventually turned into stone.

Specialist fossil-hunters—human paleontologists—look at ''recent'' fossils, made over the past 10 million years, from the time when our ape ancestors first walked on Earth. Compared with the three billion (that is, three thousand million) years of total fossil history, 10 million years is like the blinking of an eye.

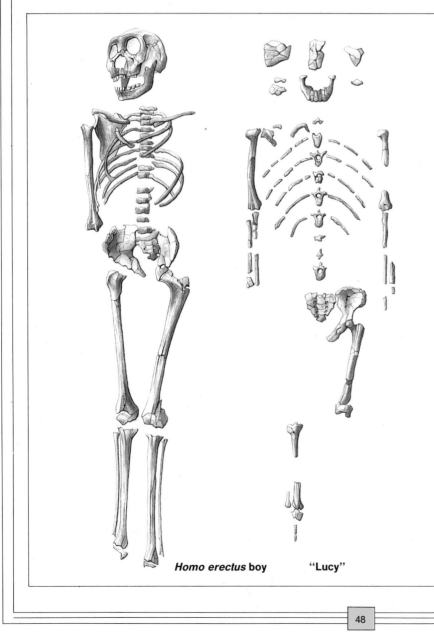

Homo erectus boy   **''Lucy''**

EARLY HUMAN SKELETON FOSSILS
The illustrations show two of the most famous sets of human skeleton fossils yet found.

The ''apewoman'' nicknamed Lucy (left) lived three million years ago in what is now north-central Ethiopia. Lucy was not a member of our own species but she belonged to a now-extinct species called by the tongue-twisting name of *Australopithecus afarensis*, which was an early branch of our complex family tree.

The bone fossils were found by a team of American scientists who investigated the rocks there in 1974. The name Lucy came from a Beatles' song, ''Lucy in the Sky with Diamonds,'' which was played all the time at the scientists' campsite.

The fossil skeleton on the far left is of a boy who lived about one and a half million years ago. He belonged to a closely related species of apelike humans which may well have been our direct ancestors. These people were called *Homo erectus*—Upright Man—because they were fully adapted for walking on two legs as we are.

This fossil was found in 1984 near Lake Turkana in Kenya, by the Kenyan fossil expert, Kamoya Kimeu.

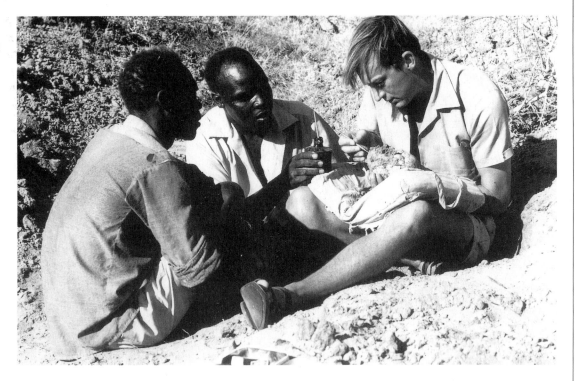

The Leakeys are a family of famous paleontologists working in Africa. Here is Richard Leakey examining an early human skull found in Kenya.

53

When did they live?

The early humans lived from about four million years ago, or perhaps earlier. We cannot be any more accurate than that.

A major problem with dating our origins has to do with the few complete fossils that we have. Animals and people that die on the land are usually eaten by scavenging animals, or their bones get broken up, leaving nothing to fossilize. Most bodies that do remain in one piece are buried in leaf litter or soil, and then soil microbes, fungi, and small invertebrates such as worms soon cause the bodies to rot away completely. Those which are quickly covered in sediments which do not encourage decay stand the best chance of becoming fossils.

Since our fossil history is based on very few fossils, scientists often cannot be sure about how long a particular early human was in existence. The absence of a fossil from a certain period of prehistory might just mean that no fossils were formed then.

Another difficulty with dating has to do with the complicated story of our evolution. The fossils that have been discovered provide many different possible origins for our present species. Over the past four million years, several humanlike apes have existed and then become extinct. It is difficult for scientists to work out the exact family links: how one species evolved from another, which species became extinct, and which evolved into a later species. Two theories are illustrated on the left: in one, we evolved from *Homo erectus* (top), in the other from *Homo habilis* (bottom).

WHO DID WE EVOLVE FROM?

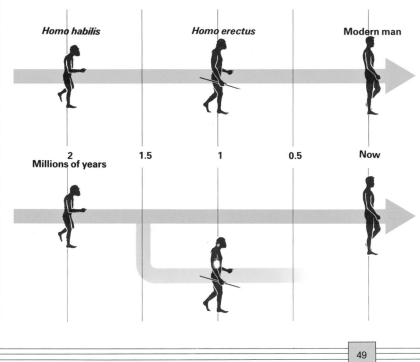

Did the first people look like us?

In some ways they were beginning to, although they still had many apelike features. Fossil experts are skilled at working out what an animal looks like from the fossil bones that it leaves behind. Their reconstructions have been used to produce "identikit" pictures of what we think the early man-apes and humans looked like.

Fossilized bones have markings on them which show where muscles and tendons were once attached. This means that the paleontologist can "reconstruct" those soft tissues and work out what the animal might have looked like in life. (Police forensic scientists use the same technique in gruesome cases where the skeleton of a long-dead murder victim is found, and they need to produce a description.)

The main characters in the four-million-years-long story of our origins are the advanced man-ape, Handy Man, Upright Man, and modern-day humans.

Some kinds of man-ape were much shorter than a modern person, being only about 3–4 ft (1–1.5 m) tall and weighing about 65 lb (30 kg). In many ways, they looked like an upright chimpanzee. They were probably hairy and dark-skinned and their faces resembled that of an ape, with big eyebrow ridges and a flattened nose.

Some kinds of Handy Man were much taller, standing about 5 ft (1.5 m) in height. This species had a larger brain than the man-apes that came before them; this is judged on the size of the fossilized skulls.

Upright Man had an even bigger body and brain than Handy Man, being 5–6 ft (1.5–1.8 m) tall, and weighing 90–160 lb (40–75 kg). These people were beginning to look remarkably like modern humans, although the face shape was different. Upright Man's brain was midway in size between that of Handy Man and our own.

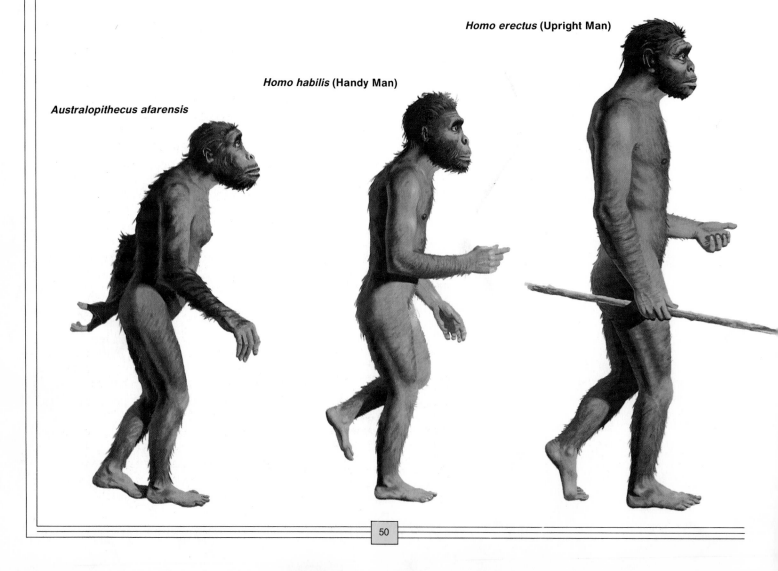

Homo erectus (Upright Man)

Homo habilis (Handy Man)

Australopithecus afarensis

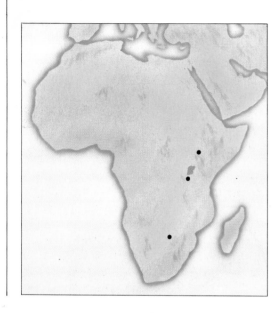

The map shows where *Homo habilis* (Handy Man) lived in Africa. Fossils of this early human species have been found at each of the sites marked. The middle one is the famous Olduvai Gorge in Tanzania.

Homo sapiens (modern man)

Where did the first humans live?

These four drawings show important landmarks in the evolution of modern people. On the far left is the tiny ***Australopithecus afarensis***, the man-ape species to which "Lucy" belonged. The remaining three are all named together in the same group, ***Homo***, which includes ourselves. ***Homo habilis*** is an early species from Africa that certainly used tools. ***Homo erectus*** was the first human species to spread out of Africa into the rest of the Old World. ***Homo sapiens*** is our own species, which seems to have first walked on the planet about 300,000 years ago.

The only way we can work out where ancient humans lived is to plot where their fossils and tools have been discovered and can still be found under the ground today. When all this information is carefully mapped, scientists can begin to have a clear picture of where we originated.

It seems certain that we began in Africa, since the remains of our early *Australopithecus* relatives have all been found in the continent of Africa. There is even direct evidence that our ancestors were walking upright on two legs on the plains of what is now Tanzania millions of years in the past. In 1976, scientists working with Dr Mary Leakey in Tanzania found two long tracks of man-ape footprints made by an adult and a child nearly four million years ago. They were walking side by side over freshly-laid, volcanic ash which then hardened.

Homo habilis (Handy Man) is known from fossils found in East Africa and southern Africa, and there is no clear evidence that these early humans ever reached Asia. *Homo erectus* (Upright Man) also seems to have evolved in the African continent, but these peoples certainly spread farther afield in small groups, in search of food supplies and shelter. We know that they reached eastern Asia and Southeast Asia from fossils, including the famous "Peking Man" and "Java Man;" they probably also lived in southern Europe.

By 300,000 years ago, Upright Man had evolved into a new species. Most scientists believe that this was an early version of modern humans. An example of such an early *Homo sapiens* fossil is the back half of a female skull found at Swanscombe, near London in the UK. The early fossil examples of our own species show that they lived in all the places where Upright Man had reached.

More modern versions of our species, including the famous "Neanderthal Man," are best known from Europe and the Middle East. The movement of modern humans to all the other parts of the world has happened very recently. The Americas did not see any humans until about 40,000 years ago, at the earliest. In fact many experts think that the first North American colonists arrived only 12,000 years ago.

Who was Neanderthal Man?

"Neanderthal Man" is the name given to a particular type, often called a sub-species, of early man. The Neanderthals seem to have developed about 200,000 years ago, from an early type of *Homo sapiens* such as the Swanscombe skull. They lived for about 170,000 years and died out around 30,000 years ago.

Every species of animal may be divided into sub-species, which are slightly different versions of a particular animal type, or species. They have small bodily differences but can nevertheless cross-breed with each other and produce young.

Our own species may have had sub-species in the past, and, if so, the most famous of these is Neanderthal Man. Most popular descriptions of these ancient people have made them out to be crude, unintelligent, violent cavemen. The truth is

very different. When they first evolved from earlier types of *Homo sapiens*, the Neanderthals were the smartest and most successful humans around. For many thousands of years they represented the highest achievement of human progress.

Neanderthals got their name from the Neander Valley near Dusseldorf in Germany. Here, the first good fossil skeleton of these ancient people was found in a cave beside the River Neander. Similar fossils have since been discovered all over Europe, as well as Israel and Iraq.

Neanderthal humans were quite varied in appearance and changed slowly over the thousands of years that they existed. But they all showed certain features which enabled them to be distinguished from the "modern" *Homo sapiens* type, to which we belong.

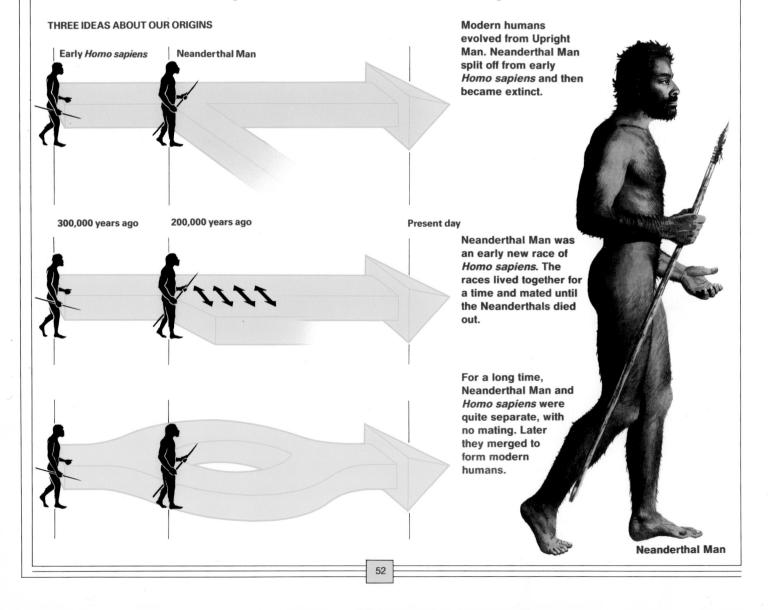

THREE IDEAS ABOUT OUR ORIGINS

Early *Homo sapiens*   Neanderthal Man

300,000 years ago   200,000 years ago   Present day

Modern humans evolved from Upright Man. Neanderthal Man split off from early *Homo sapiens* and then became extinct.

Neanderthal Man was an early new race of *Homo sapiens*. The races lived together for a time and mated until the Neanderthals died out.

For a long time, Neanderthal Man and *Homo sapiens* were quite separate, with no mating. Later they merged to form modern humans.

Neanderthal Man

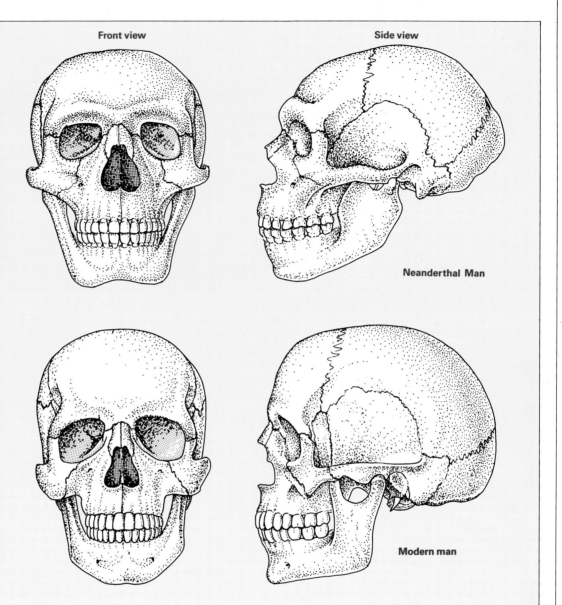

Front view

Side view

COMPARING SKULLS
The front and side views of the skulls of Neanderthal Man and Modern man show some of the key differences between them. These enable fossil hunters to say whether the skulls or pieces of skulls that they dig up come from one or the other.

The Neanderthal skull has a thick bone covering and room for an extra-large brain. The braincase is long, not domed, with a bulge at the back of the head. The Neanderthal eyebrow ridges are large and the cheekbones high and curved. Viewed from the side, you can see that Neanderthal Man had a backward-sloping forehead and a receding chin.

Modern man's skull has a domed, rounded braincase containing a smaller brain. There is no bulge at the back of the head and the cheekbones are low and straight. There is a proper chin.

Neanderthal Man

Modern man

Were Neanderthals our ancestor?

There is not an easy answer to this question, because there are big gaps in what we know about the early history of modern human beings. There was a long period, including cold Ice Age winters, when several types of humans existed in the world at the same time. There were older sorts of *Homo sapiens* that arose before the Neanderthals, and there were non-Neanderthal humans as well as the Neanderthals themselves. After they became extinct 30,000 years ago, only one sort of *Homo sapiens* was left, the same creature as ourselves.

We cannot yet tell whether these various types of early humans mated together and had children or whether they fought against each other. If Neanderthals were always very separate from other types, fought with them, and never got together with them to produce young, it could be that modern people out-competed the Neanderthals and made them extinct.

It is just as possible that in different parts of the world the Neanderthals interbred with other human types. So the "disappearance" of the Neanderthals 30,000 years ago could simply have been due to a merging of the two different lines of human evolution.

When was fire first used?

The earliest record of the use of fire may well come from two and a half million years ago: fire-scorched ground was discovered near Lake Turkana in Kenya, next to some fossil remains which helped with the dating. It is not known for certain whether early man-ape species or the early human species were the first animals on Earth to tame and to use fire.

Their use of fire was important to ancient human technology—and just as vital as electricity supplies and piped water are to us today. No non-human animal makes use of fire, and wild animals are almost always terrified of it.

The early humans who are known to have mastered fire were various groups of *Homo erectus* around the world. At a few sites where these people lived, dating between 1.6 million and 200,000 years ago, we find evidence of organized fires. Sometimes the remains are a ring of stones (for wind protection) inside which are found ashes and pieces of charred wood. At one *Homo erectus* site in northern China it has been suggested that the same "fire-place" was used for tens of years, perhaps over many generations.

The idea of fires could originally have been started from vegetation set alight by lightning strikes or by lava or hot ash from volcanic eruptions. These chance fire-lighting episodes would have given early humans the opportunity to become skilled at keeping fires alight and controlling

A rock painting from the Tassili Plateau, Algeria, shows prehistoric people hunting wild cattle with bows and arrows.

them. Only later, perhaps, did this develop into ways of starting new fires on purpose, by transporting already-smoldering logs to a new place, or by creating a spark.

The controlled use of fire would have given huge advantages to the early human groups that made them, particularly during the cold Ice Age periods. Fires would have provided heat in cold weather, and they would have warded off large animals that stalked humans at night.

A throwing stick—a device still used by Australian Aborigines—increases the power with which a spear can be thrown. Usually the force and range of a spear throw is limited by the length of a person's arm, from shoulder to hand-grip (right). With a throwing stick, the length of the "arm" is increased (far right). The spear can be thrown at greater speed and so travels farther.

How did ancient people get their food?

The man-ape australopithecines, the early human species like Handy Man and Upright Man, and finally our own species *Homo sapiens* show us a story of ever more complicated ways of getting food.

The "hunter-gatherer" tribes that still survive today in the dense rain forests of Amazonia, Central Africa, and the Far East give us an idea of the sorts of foods that can be easily found without farming. Fruits, nuts, berries, fungi, edible leaves and buds, tubers, roots, and bulbs from underground are all there for collecting.

If you can brave the stings, or cover yourself with protective gear, honey can be gathered from wild bees' nests. All kinds of soft-bodied and backboned animals can be eaten, such as caterpillars, worms, snails, shellfish, fish, lizards, birds and their eggs, and other small mammals. Early people might also have eaten each other!

Small creatures, such as limpets, are easily caught but it takes many of them to make a meal. Bigger prey, although much more hazardous to catch, might provide food for scores of people in a tribe for days or weeks. We know from the bones found near their encampments that early people used even the biggest animals as food. The group hunting methods of Neanderthals and early modern people were able to capture the largest mammoth.

The ways in which large animals were caught depended partly on ever-better hunting weapons. Over the past two million years the weapons of ancient people changed from throwing stones and sharpened wooden spears, through the use of spears and axes with heavy and sharp stone heads, up to the development of woven nets and arrows tipped with delicately shaped razor-edged stone tips. Other hunting methods were used too, such as pitfall traps for big game. Herds of horses or deer could also be stampeded over cliffs and then butchered.

Spearheads and arrow-tips were made from local stone. Compare the spearhead (1), the slate arrow-tip (2), and the quartz arrow-tip (3).

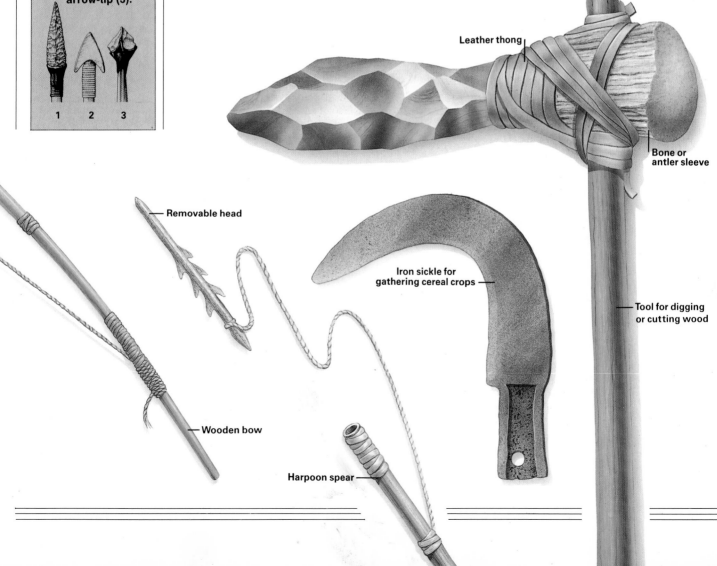

Leather thong

Bone or antler sleeve

Removable head

Iron sickle for gathering cereal crops

Tool for digging or cutting wood

Wooden bow

Harpoon spear

1 2 3

What were the first tools?

Although tools were so important to the lives of early humans, it is difficult to be sure what tools were developed first. Those left behind along with human fossils are almost always made of stone. It is quite possible that other tools were being carved from wood, bone, horn, or made from hide, vines, or other soft materials, but they would not have survived.

There is no clear evidence that the australopithecines made stone tools, although they may have done. But finds near the remains of *Homo habilis*, who lived between two million and one and a half million years ago, show that these people built simple shelters and made simple stone tools—their name in fact means Handy Man. The tools found are made from chipped rocks of basalt (lava) or quartz. The rounded stones often have one sharp edge, suggesting that they might have been used as choppers or scrapers.

Upright Man, who came after Handy Man, improved on these basic stone tools by new stone-fashioning methods. These allowed more complicated, long, jagged edges to be made on hand axes.

Neanderthal people developed even further the "toolkit" that can be made from flaked stones. A bewildering number of different stone tools from this time have been discovered, including: long, sharp, triangular points that were perhaps lashed to a wooden stick to make a lethal, heavy spearhead; and the first "knives," with one long, sharp edge that might have been used for butchering animal flesh for food or cutting up hides.

Other pieces have been identified as scrapers for cleaning hides, and jagged-edged saws for cutting wood. Stones with sharp-edged, round notches in them could have been used for smoothing tree branches into spear shafts or arrows.

The modern form of *Homo sapiens*, dating from a period stretching from 40,000 until 10,000 years ago—that is, before farming began—brought the working of stone and horn to a peak of perfection. These humans made exquisitely constructed knives, scrapers, grinding tools, arrowheads and blades, as well as harpoons and fish hooks.

HOMO SAPIENS TOOLKIT

The early forms of *Homo sapiens* known as Cro-Magnon made a wider and more finely crafted range of knives than the Neanderthals before them. Left: knife with curved back; right: knife with blunted back.

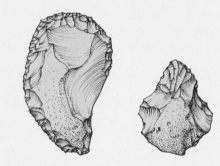

Scrapers such as the side scraper (left) and the "nosed" scraper (right) were used for cleaning hides to use as clothing and shelters.

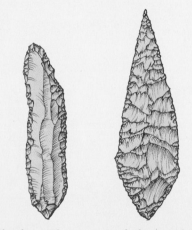

Blades for cutting were made from various kinds of rock, such as quartz or flint, and in many shapes, such as the pointed blade (left) and the laurel-leaf blade (right).

How were early tools made?

Modern scientific experts have found out how ancient peoples made their early tools by carefully observing the old stone implements that have been found in the ground, and by experimenting with different stone-working techniques in a practical way.

The earliest *Homo habilis* or Handy Man chipped stones were probably made simply by banging one stone with another. Those made by Upright Man show a more complicated technique: the long, sharp edges of their tools, particularly the hand axes, seem to have been made by a series of carefully spaced blows along each side of the blade. In one early and primitive method this was done with another stone and produced a wavy, coarse blade. Later, flexible bone or wood were probably used for the blows, so that the blade could be

hit without blunting it. This method gave longer, slimmer, and sharper edges to the stones.

Neanderthal Man and early modern man used sophisticated methods like "indirect hitting" and "pressure flaking" to make very precise, extra-sharp stone tools.

In indirect hitting, the stone being "carved" was formed with a chisel-shaped piece of bone or wood, which was itself hit with a "hammer stone." This made long, straight stone flakes that could then be worked on to make finer tools and weapons, like knives and arrowheads.

The final shaping method for the flakes themselves is known as pressure flaking. Pressing on the flake's edge with a sharpened, pointed tool made tiny flakes split off from the underside, giving the flake an even sharper edge.

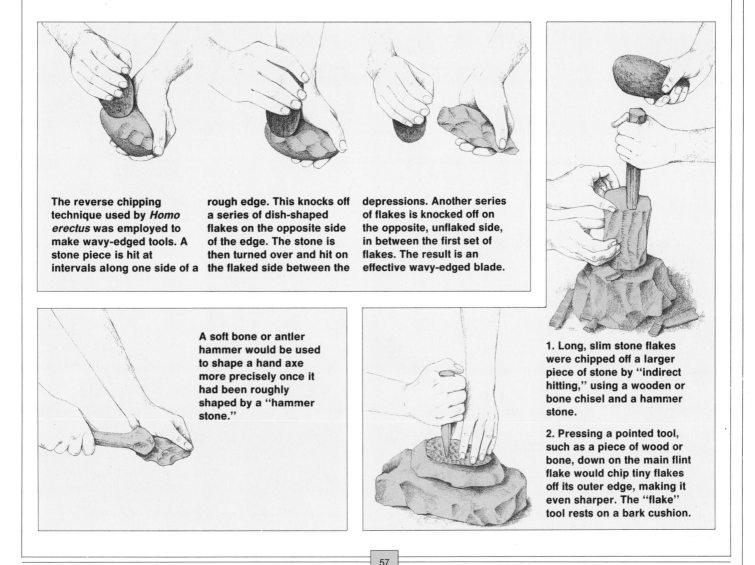

The reverse chipping technique used by *Homo erectus* was employed to make wavy-edged tools. A stone piece is hit at intervals along one side of a rough edge. This knocks off a series of dish-shaped flakes on the opposite side of the edge. The stone is then turned over and hit on the flaked side between the depressions. Another series of flakes is knocked off on the opposite, unflaked side, in between the first set of flakes. The result is an effective wavy-edged blade.

A soft bone or antler hammer would be used to shape a hand axe more precisely once it had been roughly shaped by a "hammer stone."

1. Long, slim stone flakes were chipped off a larger piece of stone by "indirect hitting," using a wooden or bone chisel and a hammer stone.

2. Pressing a pointed tool, such as a piece of wood or bone, down on the main flint flake would chip tiny flakes off its outer edge, making it even sharper. The "flake" tool rests on a bark cushion.

Why are there different races of humans?

The differences in the many races of human beings, like the variations between the sub-species of any animal, arise because living things change through time and may become altered or adapted to survive in their surroundings. The main differences are easy to spot and have to do with body build, hair and skin type and color, and the shape of the face.

Humans are distributed more widely around the world than any other backboned animal, and live in every type of surroundings imaginable. We spread all over the surface of the globe, apart from Antarctica, long before modern forms of transport were invented, and by about 10,000 years ago lived on most parts of the six continents.

Among all sorts of animals, types that spread over such long distances nearly always end up with populations specially adapted for the geographical area in which they live. These are the different sub-species, or races, of humans. You can tell from the pictures of women on the right roughly where their ancestors came from.

The color of a person's skin is a good example of this kind of adaptation. Dark brown or black skin is useful in places with strong sunshine because it stops the harmful ultraviolet rays in the sunlight from causing skin cancers. In less bright light this protection is not so important. Indeed, in low sunlight dense skin coloration (brown or black) can stop the light from making vitamin D in the skin. So, as early humans migrated from Africa, northern peoples lost much of their skin pigment, which was a barrier to sunlight, and became paler skinned. In the Tropics, there is enough light to form vitamin D even if the skin is dark.

People all over the world now travel much more than they used to, and marriages between people from different racial groups are more and more common. These changes are likely to make racial differences increasingly blurred.

Inuit (Eskimo) woman

Australian Aborigine

European woman

Masai tribeswoman, from Kenya

63

How did humans spread all over the world?

The map shows the spread of *Homo sapiens* from Africa during the last 100,000 years. By 35,000 to 40,000 years ago, modern humans had spread throughout Europe and Asia and into Australia. Possibly people came to the New World from Asia shortly afterward.

Humans of different species have spread around parts of the world at different times, but in each case the fossil evidence suggests that the new type of human developed first in Africa, before spreading to other parts of the world. For this reason, Africa has been called the "Cradle of Humankind."

The first movements happened with both the early human species *Homo erectus*, and later with *Homo sapiens*. The group of Upright Man evolved in Africa about 1.8 million years ago and later spread to eastern Asia, what is now Indonesia and, probably, Europe.

A similar pattern happened with the ancient form of *Homo sapiens*, which appears to have given rise to modern versions much like ourselves in Africa around 100,000 years ago. It is the descendants of this African-based new human type that eventually colonized the whole world and caused all the other human types that were there before, including the Neanderthals, to die out.

The evidence for this theory was based first of all on fossil bones. But more recently it has become possible for scientists to compare people's genes. The intriguing work done in this field so far confirms that Africa is indeed the likely home of all modern humankind.

Chinese girls

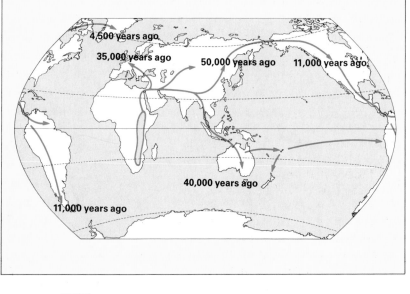

4,500 years ago

35,000 years ago

50,000 years ago

11,000 years ago

11,000 years ago

40,000 years ago

64

Did all prehistoric people live in caves?

No they did not. People often talk about prehistoric people as "cavemen," but in fact only certain types of ancient humans used caves, and only in particular places in the world and at particular times. Caves provided shelter from the weather, and protection against dangerous animals and attacks from hostile humans. But other forms of dwelling provided similar shelter where caves were not available.

Two million years ago, the group of our possible ancestors called *Homo habilis* lived in the Olduvai Gorge area in what is now Tanzania in East Africa. In the hot African climate they may have built themselves the first known human shelters. *Homo erectus* (Upright Man), who evolved in Africa about one and a half million years ago, and later spread to Asia and perhaps Europe, made shelters and used caves. Remains of oval stone and branch huts have been found on the shores of the Mediterranean and in the Pyrenees. And caves which were inhabited by *Homo erectus* have been found in China.

Later humans, called Neanderthals and Cro-Magnons, used caves and tentlike shelters, as well as fire, to help them endure the harsh, cold climate.

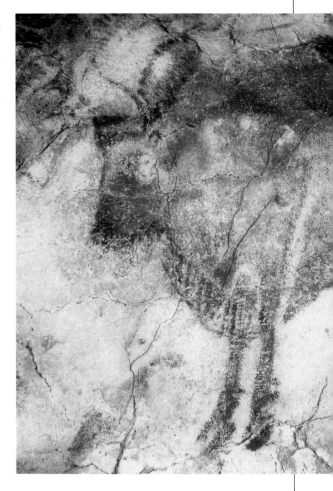

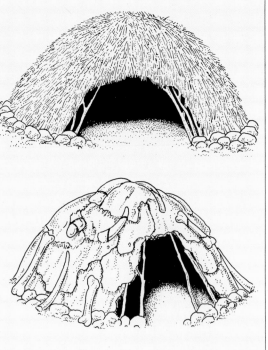

A reconstruction of the earliest prehistoric shelters is based on excavated finds of old stone circles in East Africa. The covering was probably an igloo-shape made of leafy branches.

Some Neanderthal people built outdoor huts for shelter from a branch framework covered with animal skins, weighted down with heavy mammoth bones.

65

Where can prehistoric cave paintings be found?

The most famous and best preserved cave paintings produced by prehistoric people are found in Europe. Some of the most beautiful and carefully painted caves are found at Altamira in northern Spain and at Lascaux and Pech-Merle (see examples above and right) in southwest France.

The European paintings were executed by Cro-Magnons, people belonging to the same species as ourselves (*Homo sapiens*), and done from about 25,000 to about 10,000 years ago. The least altered or damaged paintings are found on the walls and roofs of deep, dark, limestone caves. The paintings were done with charcoal or "paints" made with mineral-colored ores and soils.

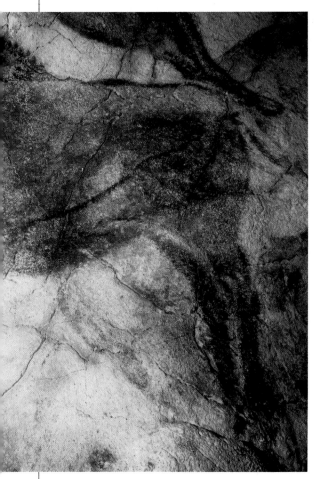

Why were they painted?

The painting of a bison is from the caves at Altamira, northern Spain.

We can only guess why the minds of the Cro-Magnons led them to paint the wonderful pictures discovered in Europe.

Many of the paintings are of the animals these early peoples hunted as food—mammoths, deer, bison, horses, seals, and fishes. Sometimes the paintings show animals actually being hunted—they have spears or arrows in their bodies and there are human figures in the pictures carrying these hunting weapons. Perhaps these hunting scenes were a sort of rehearsal of group hunting methods. Or possibly they were a type of magical or religious picture which was thought to boost the luck of the hunters on the next foray.

Certain pictures are more strange and imaginary, and show figures which are part-human, part-animal. One looks as though it has human back legs and a stag's front end. They could be either of a man dressed in skins to look like an animal or of a made-up animal–human creature. Other paintings are composed of curving squiggles, spotted patterns, geometrical shapes, or carefully lined-up rows of dots. We have no accurate idea what they mean—perhaps they are simply Cro-Magnon doodles.

The spotted horse and woolly mammoth come from the Peche-Merle paintings, France.

67

When did people first become farmers?

Farming started about 10,000 years ago, and its discovery transformed the lives of our ancestors. It began as the world moved out of the cold Ice Age. At around this time the glaciers and ice caps began to melt, the sea level rose, and areas which had once been either barren desert or tundra became grasslands or forests. In this gentler climate, a few groups of early humans taught themselves how to cultivate plant crops for eating, and to domesticate food animals.

For the 4 million years before that, australopithecine man-apes and earlier species of humans were "hunter-gatherers." That is to say, they had a very mixed diet based on the small and large animals they could hunt and all the edible plants they could gather (see Question 59). To live in this way meant being constantly on the move, following herds of animals, and seeking out trees and bushes in fruit.

The change to a farming way of life started only in a very few fertile areas. Other groups of people kept to the hunter-gatherer means of existence, and some—like the Pygmy people in Central African jungles and the Amazonian Amer-Indians—are still hunter-gatherers today.

Primitive methods of farming, using animals instead of machines, are still employed in developing parts of the world.

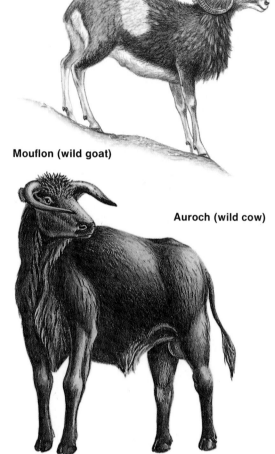

Mouflon (wild goat)

Auroch (wild cow)

Przewalski's wild horse

Red jungle fowl

Wild boar

68

What were the first farmed animals?

They were animals not unlike those of today: sheep, goats, cows, and pigs. They were tamed from wild sheep and goats, wild cattle called aurochs, and from wild boar. In Southeast Asia, the red jungle fowl was also domesticated as the chicken and became a source of meat and eggs. Goats, sheep, and cattle could feed on grass and tough vegetation that was no use as food for humans, while pigs could feed on any scraps and rubbish.

When the hunter-gatherer peoples killed adult prey animals, they must often have been able to take their young too, at an age when they were easy to control, and this may be how the first animals became domesticated. These animals were probably kept tied up or tethered and were usually poorly fed. Small-sized animals were better able to survive this treatment.

These farmed animals would have been what some scientists have called "living larders:" a source of valuable meat, fat, and hides that could be used at any time they were needed, simply by killing an animal. Their milk would also have been a useful source of food. This must have made a great difference in periods of the year when food was otherwise scarce.

69

What were the first crops?

The earliest farmed crops seem to have been a number of grasses of the types we now call cereals. There is evidence from 13,000 years ago in Israel that people were harvesting wild grass seeds as a nutritious and easily stored food, using sickles edged with sharp flints.

We guess that, from this way of life, people in different areas began to grow edible grasses deliberately, by scattering their seed on the ground near to their settlements, sowing the first crop fields. The harvest would have produced seeds to be stored for sowing the following year. Preserved seeds from early settlements show that this type of farming became common around 10,000 years ago. In the area known as the Fertile Crescent, early versions of wheat, barley, peas, and lentils were grown.

A little later—about 7,000 years ago—people in the region of China farmed millet, rice, soybeans, and yams. Later still—5,000 years ago—in the warm, wet parts of Central America, maize (sweet corn), beans, and cotton were cultivated.

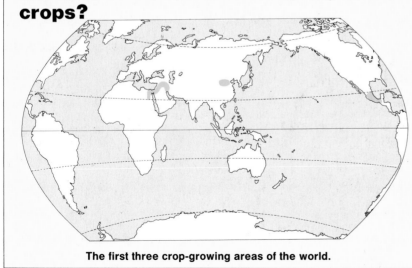

The first three crop-growing areas of the world.

Where did weeds come from?

Weeds are simply plants growing in the wrong place—any place where they are not wanted. They are a serious nuisance where crops are farmed because they can take valuable minerals from the soil, depriving the crop plant of them. They can also choke the growth of a crop plant by twining around it or by blocking the sunlight from its leaves. Some weeds are also poisonous, or they taste horrible, so if they are harvested with a crop they make it dangerous or difficult to eat.

The plants that became the weeds in the fields of the first farms, grew on our planet long before humans arrived on the scene. In the wild, these plants thrive in open places where the ground is disturbed and broken up in some way. These types of soil are found most often by river banks, on cliffs, or in sand dunes where the soil is frequently worn away.

When the first farmers cleared areas of land for crops, these intrepid weed plants would have taken hold. They would have first caused problems 10,000 years ago, when true farming began.

The most successful weeds grow rapidly, spread themselves quickly by making huge numbers of tiny seeds, or by producing spreading shoots underground, and are very hardy and tolerant of almost any type of surroundings. These are the ones that spread quickly into new areas and grow fast on newly cleared ground.

In most soils there are thousands of tiny weed seeds simply waiting underground for the present vegetation to be cleared, so that there is plenty of light. Once that happens—when a farmer cuts a crop and plows a field, for instance—the seeds can germinate, grow, flower, and make seeds in a very short time, sometimes just a week or two. They take rapid advantage of any good growing conditions.

Weed plants often have special means of making sure that their seeds get widely dispersed around the countryside in many parts of the world. The cocklebur (below) is one example. Another is the pineapple weed, a common weed found on roadsides in North America and, more recently, in Europe. Its seeds stick to mud and therefore to tractor and car tires; they have been spread far and wide this century as more and more roads are built.

THE SPREAD OF THE COCKLEBUR
Some species of weed plant have prickly seeds that spread by becoming attached to animal fur or human clothing. The cocklebur, a successful weed in warmer parts of the world, spreads by becoming dispersed in this way. The seeds or burs are covered with clinging hooked hairs, which enable them to be easily transported by animals or people. The map shows all the countries where the cocklebur has been reported as a weed.

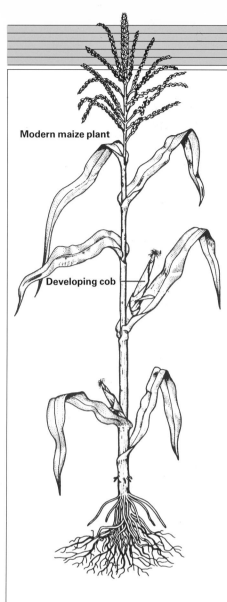

Modern maize plant

Developing cob

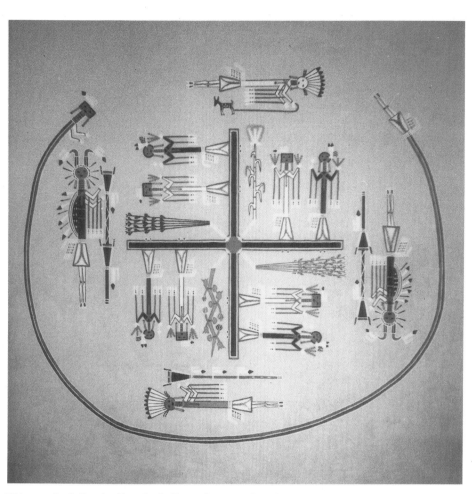

This sandpainting by Navaho Indians shows maize plants much like today's.

71

How did early farmers change wild plants into crops?

They did this by a form of "selective breeding." The skills of the hunter-gatherer peoples prepared the tribes of 10,000 years ago very well for the change to growing crops of their own. These hunter-gatherers spent a great deal of time searching for different types of plant to use as food, and they became expert at telling one type from another—it might, after all, make all the difference between enjoying a good meal and dying from food poisoning. They also learned exactly what makes particular food plants grow best. This skill helped them to search out the special places where a rare but nutritious plant grew.

The first farmers seem to have used seeds from food plants gathered in the wild as the basis for their own plantings. They cleared away existing vegetation by using tools and by burning. The ash from a fire would have provided extra nutrients in the soil for later seed growth. They

would then grow their own convenient field of food grasses—wild oats, wild wheat, and wild barley, containing a rich supply of proteins and carbohydrates in their seeds.

The crops would be cut down at harvest time and the seeds separated out to be stored as food. Some of the stored seed would be reserved for planting the following year. Simply by saving seed each year from the part of the field where the crop was of the best quality, the seed stock would be gradually improved, generation by generation.

The slow improvement of the crops with time—bigger seedheads, more seeds, less chaff and so on—was the result of "selective breeding." Each year the farmer would be choosing from among the inherited differences between the plants, and in this way slowly changing the stock to make better and better food for people.

Why did some animals become pests?

Animal pests are creatures that harm or annoy us in some way. Many of the animals that we think of as pests today began being a problem when early humans started farming.

The amount of harm pests do, and the way they operate, varies greatly. They may be biting insects that cause irritating stings or spread life-threatening diseases from person to person. They may be beetles or caterpillars which eat the crops that we grow to eat ourselves. They may be insects or small rodents such as mice that get into our larders and other food stores to munch what we have stored there.

The biting insects, such as fleas, mosquitoes, and lice, have probably lived along with human beings for a long time. They suck our blood as their own food, just as they sucked the blood of *Homo erectus* or Neanderthal people. When early humans started to cover themselves in hides to keep warm, those early clothes were a good place for some of the lice to lay their eggs. Caves and other human dwellings were also excellent shelters in which fleas could lay their eggs.

But the pests that eat crops and stored food probably only came into their own when farming and larger human settlements started, about 10,000 years ago. Before that, those animals—moths, weevils, and mice—would have lived in the wild on the seeds of grasses and on dead and rotting vegetation.

The beginnings of farmed crops, food stores, and human settlements provided these pests with a fantastic bonanza of new sources of food, as well as protection from very cold or very hot weather. Mice, rats, cockroaches, flour beetles, grain beetles, and weevils took full advantage of all the activities of early farming people, as they continue to do to this day.

Like a strange monster from science fiction, this grain weevil—hugely magnified by being viewed through a scanning electron microscope—gnaws its way out of a grain of wheat.

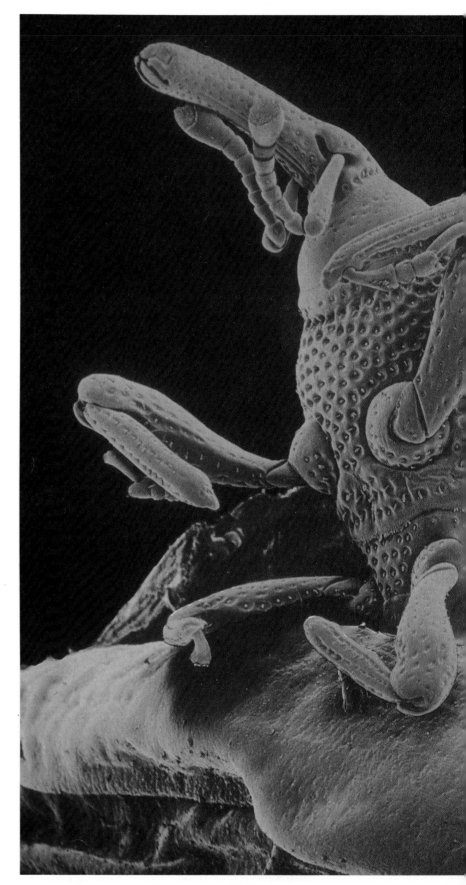

The types of animal pests that feed on stored grain and other foodstuffs are called "stored product pests." Since the beginnings of human agriculture, they have been a terrible drain on the livelihoods of farming communities. They take advantage of the huge food resource in a pile of dried grain, and can survive feeding on nothing else. Insect examples like cockroaches and flour moths lay their eggs in the food and at all stages of their life cycles—eggs, nymphs, larvae, and adults—can be found dirtying and destroying the stored food. Rats and mice are more mobile and spend time away from the stored grain, but return to it at night to feed.

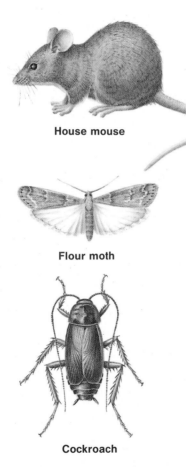

House mouse

Flour moth

Cockroach

Rat

What was the plague of locusts mentioned in the Bible?

One story told in the Book of Exodus in the Old Testament concerns the "plagues," or punishments, that the God of the Jews inflicted on the Egyptians, who would not let Moses and his people leave Egypt for the Promised Land. The account of the suffering they endured makes us realize how threatening pests must have been in the lives of the first farming communities.

> . . . and there came grievous swarms of flies into the house of Pharaoh and into his servants' houses and in all the land of Egypt the land was corrupted . . .
>   the locusts went up all over the land of Egypt . . . they covered the face of the whole Earth . . . and they did eat every herb of the land and all of the fruits of the trees . . . and there remained not any green thing, either tree or herb of the field through all the land of Egypt.

The times described in Exodus are thousands of years after farming first began in the Fertile Crescent (see Question 69). The lives of the people involved in farming had probably not changed very much since then. Plagues of pests among their crops and diseases among their farmed animals were no doubt the worst sorts of horrors that those people could imagine, and that is exactly what the Lord of the Jews caused to happen to Pharaoh and his people.

Whatever the literal truth of the story of Moses and the plagues, there is no doubt that this account has a true ring to it. It describes in a powerful way the diseases and pest outbreaks that could only happen once settled farming had begun.

Locusts today still cause great damage in parts of Africa and Asia. They migrate in huge swarms and destroy the crops over which they fly, just like in the Old Testament.

How did diseases begin?

Unfortunately, there has never been a time when people have been disease-free. All animals have diseases. These include diseases caused by microbes such as viruses and bacteria, and others like malaria, caused by parasitic creatures living in the animal's body. Humans are no different from other animals in this way.

Infectious diseases usually spread between the animals of one species—you sneeze, for example, and the person next to you catches your cold. Some infectious diseases can also pass between closely related species—which is how new species get their infections.

The modern line of humans came from apes and apelike humans in Africa. The early stages in our evolution, from about four million years ago onward, happened in a landscape where there were also many apes and monkeys which were quite closely related to ourselves. We almost certainly caught some of our early diseases by cross-infections from those distant cousins.

The evidence of those past links can still be seen today. Diseases like yellow fever and malaria, which are spread between people by mosquito bites, can also infect gorillas and chimpanzees. We probably caught them from animals like those in the first place.

Other types of diseases, for example "tummy bugs" like *Salmonella*, which are caused by bacteria, are passed from animal to animal when water contaminated by their droppings is drunk. We probably originally became infected with such diseases when, many thousands of years ago, we shared water holes in Africa with a range of other animals.

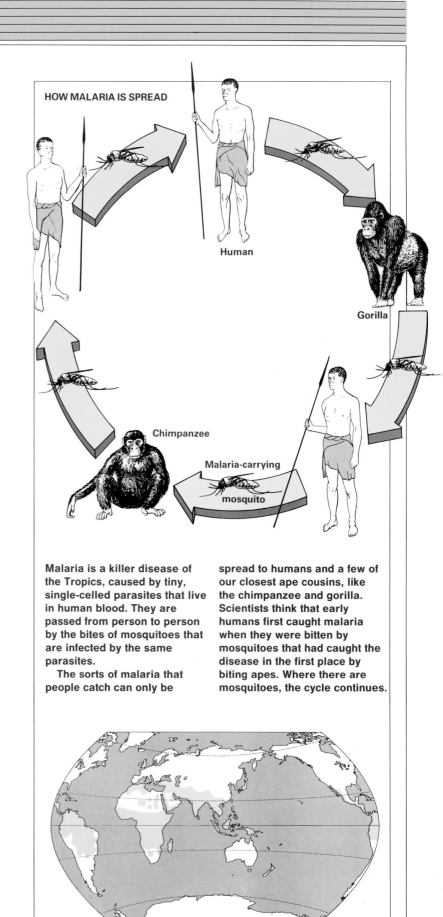

HOW MALARIA IS SPREAD

Human

Gorilla

Chimpanzee

Malaria-carrying mosquito

Malaria is a killer disease of the Tropics, caused by tiny, single-celled parasites that live in human blood. They are passed from person to person by the bites of mosquitoes that are infected by the same parasites.

The sorts of malaria that people catch can only be spread to humans and a few of our closest ape cousins, like the chimpanzee and gorilla. Scientists think that early humans first caught malaria when they were bitten by mosquitoes that had caught the disease in the first place by biting apes. Where there are mosquitoes, the cycle continues.

THE DISTRIBUTION OF MALARIA IN THE TROPICS

Do we get the same diseases as ancient peoples?

Some are the same and some are very different. We still share some ancient tropical diseases like malaria with non-human apes to this day. These must have been the same diseases as our early hunter-gatherer ancestors suffered from in the continent of Africa.

The diseases affecting us probably changed when early man—*Homo erectus* and *Homo sapiens*—first left Africa and moved around the world. When they arrived in cooler zones, our ancestors left behind many of the insects like tropical mosquitoes that spread diseases between people. They also left behind other species of monkeys and apes, none of which live outside the Tropics. This meant they could no longer catch diseases from other apes. However, African peoples today still suffer from malaria, and westerners are also at risk whenever they visit tropical countries.

When farming started and more people started living together, around 10,000 years ago, we started to catch new diseases from the animals we had domesticated and lived close to. Today we share over 50 diseases with dogs, for instance.

The greatest problems came when large numbers of people started living together. Many sorts of infectious diseases cannot survive in small, constantly moving groups of people because the disease organisms simply never meet enough people to infect. But those same diseases can, in closely packed towns or cities, turn into horrific epidemics of illnesses. Diseases such as influenza, tuberculosis, cholera, typhoid, plague, and smallpox only became a serious threat once large towns and cities developed.

Cholera is a dangerous human disease caused by bacteria. It is transferred from person to person when they drink water that is contaminated by the feces of other infected people. It becomes a serious problem in communities of a large size, such as towns and cities, and in which sanitation (hygienic water supplies and drainage systems) is poor, as it was everywhere before this century.

New diseases are still arising, all the time. AIDS, for instance, a killing virus disease that destroys a patient's immune system, only began to infect people in the 1960s and 1970s. Like so many of the diseases we first caught from our ape and monkey cousins, millions of years ago, AIDS seems to have developed from a monkey-based virus.

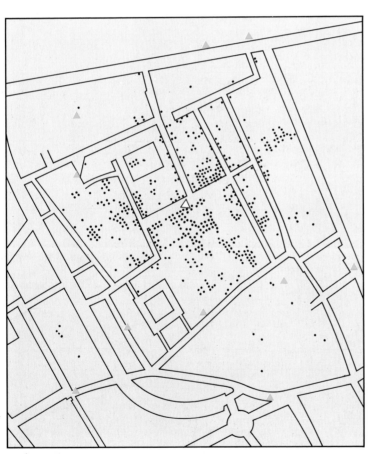

▲ Water pump

∷ Deaths from cholera

The map shows details of one of the first cholera epidemics whose origins were properly understood. In the 1850s there were many cholera outbreaks in London, where the population was dense and the sanitation poor. This outbreak in the Soho area was traced to a public water pump in Broad Street (the central triangle on the map). The drinking water at this pump was fouled by a broken underground cesspit, containing untreated sewage. This explained why the deaths were clustered around the site of the street water pump.

What were the first pets?

A pet is an animal—like a cat, rabbit, dog, or gerbil—that is kept in your home as a companion to the family: a sort of animal friend. Keeping a pet animal, one which does not have to "work for its living" in the household, is a very recent idea, dating back to the last few hundred years, and only practised in rich and developed countries. Even today, pets are a luxury that cannot be afforded in poor, developing countries where food for people is in short supply.

The first animals that were kept by early humans and not simply used as a source of meat (see Question 68) were probably dogs. There is evidence that by about 13,000 years ago early peoples in the Fertile Crescent area of southwest Asia had tamed the wild wolf cubs that lived there and turned them into the first domesticated dogs. These dogs would have had many uses, apart from being companion animals (see next question).

The earliest evidence of cats being associated with humans is in the Egyptian tomb paintings of 3,500 years ago. Cats were almost worshipped by the Egyptian peoples, although their only practical use in a home would have been in controlling pests such as mice and rats.

The dingo is the only mammal in Australia that is neither a primitive egg-layer, like the platypus, nor a pouched mammal (marsupial), like the kangaroos and wombats. It is thought that the dingo was brought to Australia thousands of years ago, as a sort of tame dog, when Aborigine peoples trekked from Asia to Australia.

This section of a carved relief from the walls of an Assyrian palace at Nineveh, dating from 2,600 years ago, shows huntsmen with tame dogs.

What use were pets to early humans?

Dogs and cats have both been "adopted" by people during the last 13,000 years. But unlike sheep, goats, cattle, and pigs, they have hardly ever been used as food animals. They have almost always carried out certain tasks for the early humans who took them into their homes.

The usefulness of dogs has meant that they were soon found in most human cultures around the world. Perhaps, to begin with, they were used as fast, strong helpers with a powerful sense of smell during human hunting trips. A group of dogs working with humans would have made a fearsome hunting team.

The dogs could have stampeded herds of prey animals over cliffs or toward hidden hunters with weapons. They might have fetched birds and other small game brought down by arrows, or even been used directly to attack and bring down larger prey animals. Wild hunting dogs in Africa today can kill animals much larger than themselves by attacking in groups.

The early tame dogs had other uses too. They could have guarded flocks and herds of farmed animals from the attacks of large predators, or been used for herding and controlling them just as a shepherd uses a sheepdog today. They could also protect homes, by barking whenever predators or enemies approached.

Cats were used in different ways. They came to be regarded almost as gods by some of the Ancient Egyptians. Many beautiful stone and bronze statues of sitting cats have been found in Egyptian excavations—some with gold earrings in their ears! Cats were even turned into miniature animal mummies.

One possible reason these cats were given such special treatment was the importance of their job as exterminators. The fertile soils along the banks of the River Nile produced large grain harvests, and excess grain was stored to be eaten during the winter. These grain stores would attract hordes of hungry rats and mice, but tamed cats would keep down their numbers by killing them. By guarding the granary in this way, they were rewarded by being very well looked after.

Could prehistoric people speak?

Yes, they probably could speak, although it seems possible that this important stage was not reached until the man-apes—the australopiths—changed into the early humans known as *Homo*.

The evidence we have for thinking that prehistoric people could speak is pieced together from fossil clues. Paleontologists—fossil scientists—have used fossil skulls as molds to make impressions of the surface of the brains once inside them. We know from this that the australopith brains did not have the bulges known to be involved with the use of speech (shown right), but later *Homo* species did.

No one is quite sure exactly when, over the past two million years since *Homo* first walked on Earth, the spoken word really began. Even though the brain bulges were there in the early humans, the voice-box (the larynx, with its vocal cords) may not have been complicated enough to make all the sounds that we can produce today. It seems likely that simple speech began around two million years ago. Groups that could communicate better, because of their use of speech, would have been more successful than those with only basic forms of communication, such as grunts.

SPEECH-CONTROL IN THE BRAIN
There are two special bulges on the left-hand side of the brain that we now know are linked with the use of speech. One is needed for the control of the delicate movements of the lips, tongue, cheeks, and voice-box in the throat that are needed to make words. The other is required for understanding what a spoken word means.

The impressions made of the brains of *Homo habilis* and *Homo erectus*, as well as those of our own species, *Homo sapiens*, show clear signs of these two crucial, one-sided bulges.

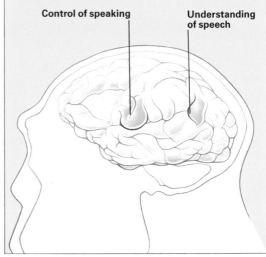

Control of speaking   Understanding of speech

Sign language is a special form of communication for people who are deaf and dumb. It has its own rules and grammar.

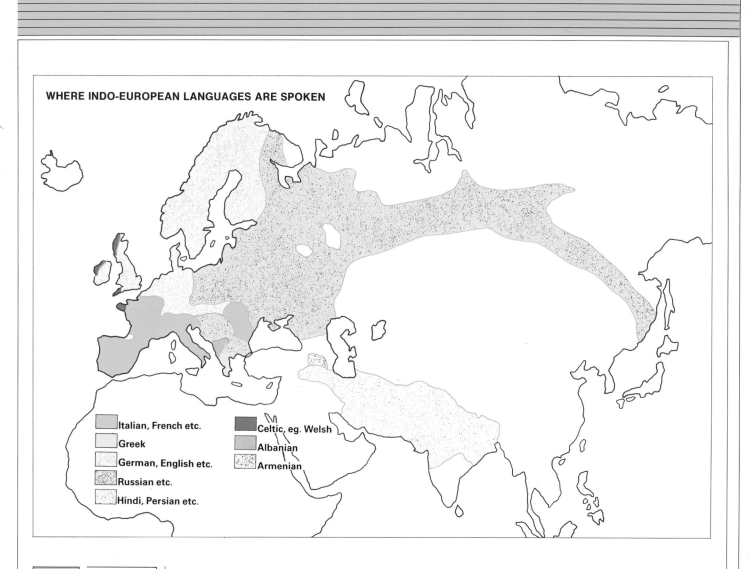

WHERE INDO-EUROPEAN LANGUAGES ARE SPOKEN

Italian, French etc.

Greek

German, English etc.

Russian etc.

Hindi, Persian etc.

Celtic, eg. Welsh

Albanian

Armenian

79

Why do different people speak different languages?

People from different lands speak different languages because human speech has become something that varies from place to place on the Earth's surface. In some ways it is like skin color (see Question 60), except that language, unlike skin color, is not inherited (passed down in the genes from one generation to another). It is a skill that is learned.

What all human babies get from their parents is the incredibly skilful ability to pick up the language that is being used around them as they grow up. If you take a baby from anywhere in the world and move it at birth to a new country, it will grow up learning the local language as easily as the local children. It will not instinctively know its "own" language.

As ancient people moved around the world, settled in different areas and set up tribes, bigger groups of tribes, and eventually nations, they took their language with them. In the past, when

long-distance travel was much more difficult than it is today, tribes and nations were very isolated from each other. This meant that languages easily became split up into local versions or "dialects."

If you study those languages carefully— both the words that they use (the vocabulary) and the rules for putting the words together in meaningful ways (the grammar)—it is found that the world's languages can be sorted into some large families. Each family of languages is thought to be the group of local versions of a single, ancient basic language that is no longer used by anyone.

English, for instance, belongs to a family of languages which experts have called "Indo-European." The original language family spread through much of Europe and many parts of southern Asia and seems to have been spoken in most of this region more than 5,000 years ago, before splitting up into local languages.

Who were the Ancient Egyptians?

Ancient Egypt was a civilization that began around 5,000 years ago in the north-east corner of Africa, and lasted for about 3,000 years. It was rich and successful and the remains of its many treasures, temples, and cities have told us a great deal about life in those times.

The country of Ancient Egypt was dependent on the River Nile in every way. The area in which people lived was a narrow strip of land about 600 miles (1,000 km) long on either side of the Nile. The river flooded every year, spreading fertile mud, or silt, over the land. This nourishment, and the Nile's irrigating waters enabled good crops to be grown along the river banks. These farming opportunities led to a well-organized civilization growing up around the Nile.

81

What is a mummy?

An Egyptian mummy is the artificially preserved body of an Ancient Egyptian— usually a king or nobleman. The dead body was protected and preserved in this way so that he could live forever.

The making of a mummy was a long and sacred task, carried out by high priests. The king's internal organs were carefully removed, and placed in preservative salts and oils in four special, stoppered jars or mini-coffins. The rest of the body was placed in preservatives and wrapped in linen bandages before being clothed in rich garments and jewelry.

The mummy was then placed in a richly carved, body-shaped coffin, encrusted with gold and precious stones. Often there was a series of these coffins—one inside the other like giant Russian dolls—so that the mummy inside was very well protected. This was then put in a heavy stone vault called a sarcophagus, with a stone lid.

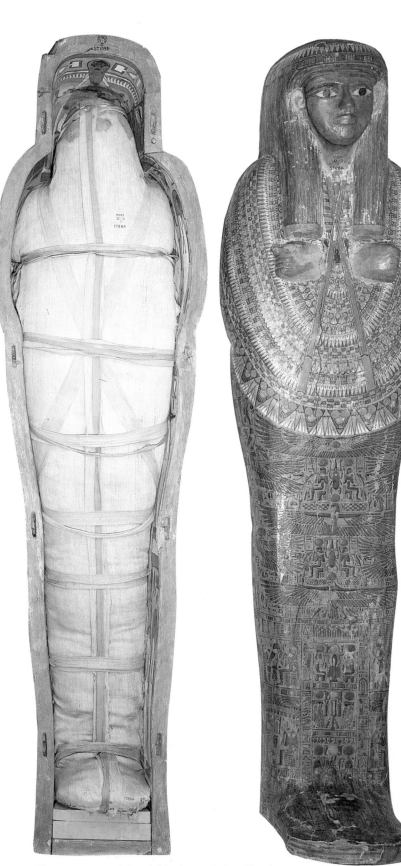

The mummy and the richly decorated coffin of an unnamed priestess, from the ancient city of Thebes, 1050 B.C.

A painting from the tomb of an Egyptian nobleman shows a table piled high with all the provisions for the afterlife.

82

Why were mummies buried with furniture, food, and drink?

The reasons why mummies in Ancient Egypt were buried with many household items has to do with the religious thinking that was behind the making of a mummy in the first place. Even in life, the king or pharaoh was thought of as a god. In death—provided the correct rituals and spells were carried out—it was believed that he would become Osiris, god of the Underworld, and would live forever.

Consequently, the Ancient Egyptians thought that in the magical afterlife the god-king would need all the objects that a living king would need in his former life. This is why the burial places of the pharaohs (when they have not been plundered) were found to contain the wonderful collections of household objects that have taught us so much about the everyday life of Egyptian nobles.

In the tomb of the pharaoh Tutankhamun, almost the whole buried treasure survived until it was excavated this century. Among the thousands of objects found were several full-sized chariots with harnesses, as well as extravagantly decorated thrones, seats, beds, desks, and storage chests. Smaller, more personal items included a board game, a painting palette, a fan, a trumpet, a hunting bow, and a boomerang for hunting birds. The pharaoh certainly had all he needed for a full and interesting life in the Kingdom of the Dead.

Why were the pyramids built?

The three pyramids at Giza, in Egypt. The Great Pyramid in the middle was built out of two and a half million cubic limestone blocks, each weighing about 2.5 tons. The original facing of shiny white limestone can today only be seen near the top. There would also once have been a gold cap stone at the pyramid's tip.

Pyramid-shaped stone monuments have been built by many ancient civilizations. They were usually intended as impressive temples to the gods or the tombs of rulers.

The oldest known pyramid is the flat-topped "Ziggurat," or temple tower, built in the ancient city of Ur (in what is now Iraq) about 5,500 years ago. It is thought to have been built as a temple, to resemble the mountains on which the gods lived.

The early Egyptian pyramids were step-sided structures, built to suggest a majestic stairway for the king's spirit to join the sun god. The most famous of these is the large step pyramid built at Saqqara, south of Cairo, by King Djoser, about 4,600 years ago. It overlooked the ancient capital of Memphis. It was constructed in the middle of a huge enclosure of sacred buildings and was made out of millions of sun-dried clay bricks.

The "golden age" of sloping-sided stone pyramid buildings was the period of the Egyptian Old Kingdom (4,700 to 4,200 years ago). The pharaohs of that time all constructed huge pyramids of stone blocks as the final resting place for their mummies. These monumental structures took so long to build that they had to be started as soon as the king came to the throne, in order to be finished by the time he died.

The most famous pyramids of all are the three pyramids at Giza, to the west of Cairo. The largest of these, called the Great Pyramid, is the only one of the Seven Wonders of the Ancient World that can still be seen today. It was built by the Pharaoh Cheops, who ruled Egypt from 2589–2566 B.C.

The Great Pyramid is still the world's largest and its statistics are awe-inspiring. It is about 450 ft (150 m) high, with the base of each side about 750 ft (250 m) long. The four flat sides point accurately to the four points of the compass, while the huge base is almost perfectly level. Astonishingly, it varies in measurement by no more than 1 in (2.5 cm) from one corner to the next.

How could the pyramids be built without modern machines?

We will probably never know exactly how the Egyptian pyramids were built, but we do have many clues, which give us a good idea of the techniques and materials used by those skilful ancient builders. Tens of thousands of workmen must have been employed on these building projects. It is estimated that the Great Pyramid itself took over 5,000 workers 20 years to build.

The limestone blocks were quarried near to the construction site on the Giza plateau. The famous sphinx statue next to the pyramid is in fact built on the site of one of those quarries. The white "shiny" limestone used for facing the sides of the pyramids came from a quarry on the opposite bank of the Nile. And the granite from which the sarcophagus itself was carved came all the way from Aswan in the south of Egypt, 500 miles (800 km) away.

All this stone would have been transported to the construction site by water, with the stones carried on boats or rafts down the Nile itself, or along specially constructed canals. At the building site,

the extremely heavy stones would have been pulled over rolling poles by the large teams of workmen.

The Ancient Egyptians are known to have had great astronomical and mathematical skills, and these would have enabled them to make the pyramids face in a particular direction. They could work out due north very accurately by watching particular stars as they rose over the night-time horizon and sank beneath it. And since they understood the science of right angles, they could then make all the other sides correspond to other compass points.

The flatness of the pyramid's base was probably produced by a water-leveling method. Once the site was roughly leveled, it was flooded with water, the level of which would be perfectly flat. Then thousands of stakes could be banged into the ground until their tops just reached the water surface. When the water was let out, the tops of the stakes would show a perfectly level base for the first layer of stone building blocks.

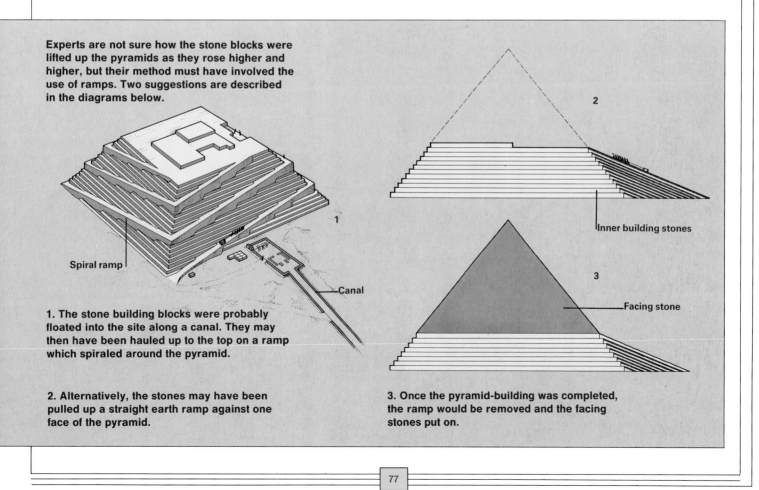

Experts are not sure how the stone blocks were lifted up the pyramids as they rose higher and higher, but their method must have involved the use of ramps. Two suggestions are described in the diagrams below.

Spiral ramp

Canal

Inner building stones

Facing stone

1. The stone building blocks were probably floated into the site along a canal. They may then have been hauled up to the top on a ramp which spiraled around the pyramid.

2. Alternatively, the stones may have been pulled up a straight earth ramp against one face of the pyramid.

3. Once the pyramid-building was completed, the ramp would be removed and the facing stones put on.

85

Who was Tutan-khamun?

The back of the royal gilt throne, decorated with a scene from Tutankhamun's private life. It shows his wife annointing him with oils under the rays of the "solar disc," the symbol of the sun god.

Tutankhamun was the most famous of all the kings of Ancient Egypt. His fame was not because he ruled the longest: he reigned for only nine years, from 1361 to 1352 B.C., and was only 18 when he died. Neither was he a great general—he did not conquer other countries as so many of the other kings or pharaohs had done.

The reason everyone knows the name of Tutankhamun is because his was the only Egyptian pharaoh's tomb ever found which had not been looted by robbers. His tomb was in the Valley of Kings, where many later pharaohs were buried in long, tunnel-shaped tombs cut in the rock walls of the majestic valley, or in its floor. When Tutankhamun's tomb was first opened in 1922, almost all its precious contents were in exactly the same state as they had been left by the high priests in charge of the burial, over 3,200 years before. Tutankhamun was buried with his two stillborn daughters.

86

How was his tomb discovered?

The discovery of Tutankhamun's tomb on 26 November 1922 was one of the most amazing archeological finds ever made.

Every Egyptian king from 1525 to 1379 B.C., as well as the two rulers who came after Tutankhamun, was buried in a tomb cut into the rock in the Valley of Kings. Their tombs had all been discovered by the end of the nineteenth century, so archeologists were sure that Tutankhamun's tomb must also be somewhere in the valley. In a long series of excavations, they had searched the valley in vain up until 1914, finding only a few figures and boxes with Tutankhamun's name on.

The British archeologist Howard Carter took over the search from 1914 and made massive excavations throughout the valley. His workmen shifted over 200,000 tons of sand and rubble over the next eight years, to expose the rock floor of the valley. But they discovered almost nothing and by the summer of 1922 had almost given up hope.

Carter and his financial supporter, Lord Carnarvon, decided to spend one more season searching at the only spot they had not cleared before. It was a pile of rubble down-slope of the entrance to the previously excavated tomb of Ramesses VI.

Almost as soon as this last dig had begun, they found a group of ancient workmen's huts, and underneath was a series of steps cut into the rocks, leading down into the valley floor. At the bottom of the steps was a doorway, plastered over and sealed with the unbroken seal of the ancient guards of the necropolis, or City of the Dead. The door also had Tutankhamun's name carved on it.

Inside was a corridor that led into a series of four rooms, one of which was the burial chamber. This held the mummy of the pharaoh, inside a solid gold coffin weighing over 220 lb (100 kg). The rooms were packed with untouched treasures which, in the dry atmosphere, had survived almost unchanged for over 3,000 years.

The magnificent funeral mask worn by the mummy of Tutankhamun. Made of solid gold, it is inlaid with semi-precious stones and glass-paste.

When did writing start?

The earliest writing for which we have records dates from over 5,000 years ago. This system of true writing, which stood for a spoken language, was used by the Sumerians. The Sumerians were a group of people living in the area called Mesopotamia, between the rivers Tigris and Euphrates, in what is now modern Iraq.

The Sumerians wrote by pressing wedge-shaped writing tools into tablets of wet clay to make an impression, then they baked the tablets. These cooked clay tablets were tough, and those buried in the ground have survived until today. The tablets have been studied and their writing, called cuneiform (meaning wedge-shaped), can now be read and understood by modern experts.

Soon after the start of cuneiform writing, a quite different type of writing was developed in Ancient Egypt, called heiroglyphic. It consisted of lines, forming simple pictures of objects like birds and insects, as well as geometrical shapes.

In both early hieroglyphs and the Sumerian wedge-shaped writing, each word was represented by an individual symbol, or by several signs: both were types of picture writing. Even today, in certain languages such as modern Chinese, some words are written as pictures.

Sumerian clay tablet with cuneiform writing (2100 B.C.)

The development of writing started with the earliest picture signs (1). Over the centuries these picture signs were turned on their sides and gradually changed, in stages:
(2) Sumerian cuneiform writing, about 2500 B.C.
(3) Early Babylonian writing, about 1800 B.C.
(4) Assyrian writing, about 700 B.C.
(5) More recent Babylonian writing, about 600 B.C.

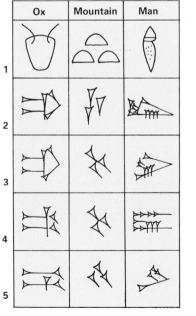

	Ox	Mountain	Man
1			
2			
3			
4			
5			

Egyptian hieroglyphs, giving the names of four kings (1270 B.C.)

see Question 92

88

How did picture writing turn into words?

The Greeks used either a waxed wooden writing tablet (left), pressing the letters in with a stylus made of bronze, ivory, or wood. Or they wrote on sheets of papyrus, using a bronze or a reed pen with a split nib.

Over a long period of time, pictures came to represent syllables—the parts in which separate segments of a word are spoken. Then the syllable-symbols gradually turned into letters, each of which stood for a basic sound.

The problem with picture writing is that thousands of different symbols have to be learned in order to write—or read—anything which is at all complicated. Modern Chinese, for instance, has about 50,000 different characters and such a written language is very difficult to learn. In ancient times it was likely that only the rulers and their high priests and scribes learned how to write such languages. Writing was not something that ordinary people could hope to learn—it was a symbol of power and position.

So an early development of the first "picture writing" languages were written languages based on syllable sounds. In later forms of Egyptian hieroglyphs, and the form of wedge-writing used in Babylon (see Question 92), the symbols stood for the sound of a syllable, rather than the whole word. Because individual syllables are common to many words, this meant that less symbols were needed to be able to write all the words in the language. Babylonian wedge-writing, for example, needed only 600 characters.

Most modern written languages, though, have gone one step further: they are based on alphabets. Alphabet languages can have an even smaller number of symbols, because each symbol or "letter" stands for a basic sound. Most alphabets around the world need only 30 or less letters —this makes them much easier to remember than thousands of word pictures.

Most modern written languages seem to have developed from a late form of Egyptian hieroglyphs which have picture-word, syllable, and alphabet meanings. Fully alphabetic writing was first developed by Middle Eastern peoples in the Sinai area around 1,000 B.C. From those roots, Hebrew, then Greek and Latin written alphabets developed.

89

Who built Stonehenge?

Stonehenge is a monument of gigantic shaped stones which stands on the windswept chalk downs of Salisbury Plain in southern England. It was built over a very long period of time, between 3,000 and 4,000 years ago, by Bronze Age people, so-called because they had discovered how to make the hard metal alloy called bronze to use in tools and containers. These Bronze Age people have been called Megalithic, meaning "large stone," for the stone monuments they left.

Although now partly ruined, the Stonehenge monument was originally a ring of huge vertical stones, each 16 ft (5 m) high and weighing about 26 tons, placed among many other circles and horseshoe patterns of standing stones. It includes the famous archway sets of three stones called "trilithons."

Some of the larger stones are made from bluestone, which can only have come from a particular rock outcrop on a hilltop in the Preseli Hills in southwest Wales, some 200 miles (320 km) away. It is thought the stone must have been floated to Stonehenge on wooden rafts.

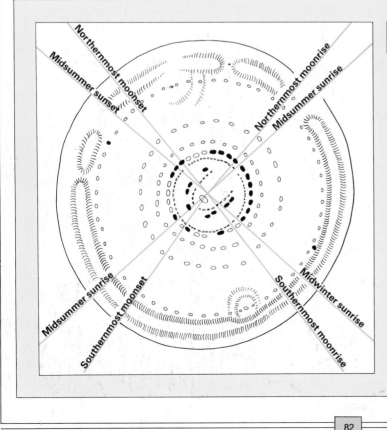

90

What was Stonehenge for?

There have been many ideas about what this stone monument was used for. It seems most likely that the Bronze Age people who built Stonehenge erected it as a temple to the gods they worshipped. But scientists have recently discovered that the many stones of Stonehenge could be lined up with the places where the Sun and Moon rose and set on particular days throughout the seasons (see left). Using this information, it is possible that the stones were used to predict eclipses.

In Bronze Age times, eclipses of the Sun or Moon would have been thought of as strange, magical, and frightening things. A priest who could say when an eclipse would happen would be considered to have magical powers.

Is Stonehenge unique?

The huge "archway" stones at Stonehenge are fitted together with carefully cut, but now hidden, ball and socket joints.

Not really. Stonehenge is doubtless one of the more complicated sets of standing stone circles from Bronze Age Europe to have survived so well, but there are other impressive "large-stone" monuments from about the same time. They are to be found in northwest Europe and also farther south in the Mediterranean region.

There is a monument at Carnac, in northern France, also built around 2,000 B.C., which consists of mysterious single standing stones called "menhirs." They are set up in parallel rows like avenues, some of them nearly a mile (over 1 km) long.

At Newgrange in Ireland is a famous "passage grave," built earlier, in about 3,200 B.C. An underground passageway leads to a stone tomb chamber, arranged to admit the Sun's rays in midwinter. The chamber was covered by a huge stone mound, surrounded by other carved stones.

The most sophisticated Megalithic monuments are packed together on the tiny island of Malta, south of Italy. Built between 3,200 and 2,500 B.C. these temple buildings are carved with spirals, geometric patterns, and farm animals.

Part of the circle of Megalithic standing stones at Avebury, in southern England.

Where was the city of Babylon?

The ancient city of Babylon was built next to the River Euphrates in southwest Asia. The Euphrates and its sister river, the Tigris, rise next to each other in the mountains south of the Black Sea and form a pair of rich and fertile valleys that stretch down to the Persian Gulf.

Babylon started as a small town in about 3000 B.C., but it first became important when a series of kings, including the famous Hammurabi (1792–1750 B.C.), made the city their capital and built a great ziggurat or stepped temple pyramid there.

This first city declined after Hammurabi died, and only began its second rise to power a thousand years later, when a new Babylonian Empire arose around 600 B.C. The second king of this Empire was Nebuchadnezzar, who conquered the Hebrews of Judah and took them into exile in his own kingdom, as described in the Book of Daniel in the Old Testament. For a time this same Nebuchadnezzar made Babylon the most fabulous and beautiful city in the world.

Were there really hanging gardens in Babylon?

Yes, there almost certainly were. The Hanging Gardens of Babylon were one of the Seven Wonders of the Ancient World, although nothing remains of them today.

The gardens are supposed to have been built on terraces in the city, irrigated with water from the River Euphrates. These "hanging" gardens would have contained flowers and all types of fruit trees, as well as palm trees. Legend has it that the gardens were built on the orders of Nebuchadnezzar, in order to remind his wife of the mountains and trees of her native land.

Small temple

An artist's impression of Nebuchadnezzar's Babylon. It was about a square mile in extent, an enormous city by the standards of that time, with the River Euphrates running through the middle of it. The city was surrounded by a vast city wall, so wide that the Greek historian, Herodotus, who visited it in about 460 B.C., said that two chariots, each drawn by four horses, could pass one another easily on top of it. Excavations on the site suggest that he was not exaggerating.

Babylon boasted many temples and magnificent gateways, all covered with blue-glazed ceramic bricks which must have shone brilliantly.

The famous Hanging Gardens

From about 5,000 years ago, the banks of the Rivers Tigris and Euphrates were the sites of a series of famous ancient cities, including Nineveh, Ashur, Ur, and Babylon itself. Looked at on today's map, the site of Babylon is near the modern town of Hilla, south of Baghdad, in Iraq.

Nineveh
R. Tigris
IRAN
Baghdad
Hilla
BABYLON
R. Euphrates
IRAQ
Ur
SAUDI ARABIA   KUWAIT

Main entrance to Babylon through the impressive Ishtar Gate, brilliantly colored and decorated

Are there still any lost civilizations?

Although it would be exciting to think that there still exist civilizations waiting to be discovered, unfortunately this is highly unlikely, outside of Indiana Jones movies. Today's advanced forms of transport and methods of detection mean that there are hardly any secret parts of the world left.

While there are still some regions of the Earth's surface that have been only poorly explored, particularly in dense rain forests, these parts have been carefully examined using aerial photography and scanning from satellites. Any lost living civilizations would show up in these pictures because of their buildings or other structures, but none have been found.

There may be a few small groups of hunter-gatherers, who have never been in contact with the modern world, still to be discovered in deep jungles. But as the rain forests are rapidly cut down, burned, and developed, even this gets more and more unlikely.

A group of Waorani Indians, a primitive tribe still living a hunter-gatherer existence in Equador, South America.

95 Was there a real place called Atlantis?

Many legends surround the lost island civilization called Atlantis throughout history, but nobody knows if it existed.

The first story about Atlantis was told by Plato, an Ancient Greek philosopher who lived about 2,400 years ago. His story, set in the far past, was that the vast island of Atlantis was bigger than Asia Minor and Libya put together and that it was situated in the Atlantic Ocean.

Plato described a flourishing civilization on the island, with great, well-planned cities and large ships used for trade and fighting. His tale told how its peoples made Atlantis the most powerful kingdom in the Mediterranean. But in the end, as they became greedy for more and more power, by fighting other nations, the gods destroyed Atlantis by directing against it natural forces, such as earthquakes and floods. The island continent of Atlantis eventually sank without trace.

Modern research shows that there might be some truth behind the legends, even though we know from detailed studies of the Atlantic sea bed that there are no remains of islands in the part of the Atlantic to which Plato was referring. But a different interpretation has begun to tie up facts with the legends.

Between 2500 and 1500 B.C., an advanced civilization did exist on the islands of the Eastern Mediterranean, especially on Crete and on the smaller island then called Thera (now Santorini) to the north of Crete. Wall paintings from Santorini show huge sea-going ships and large cities, while on Crete itself the Minoan civilization built large, well-planned cities and developed a written language.

Around 1500 B.C., these active kingdoms came to a rapid end. One of the reasons for this must have been the gigantic volcanic eruption that happened on the island of Thera about 1520 B.C.

Excavations at Santorini in Greece have unearthed remains of the Minoan civilization.

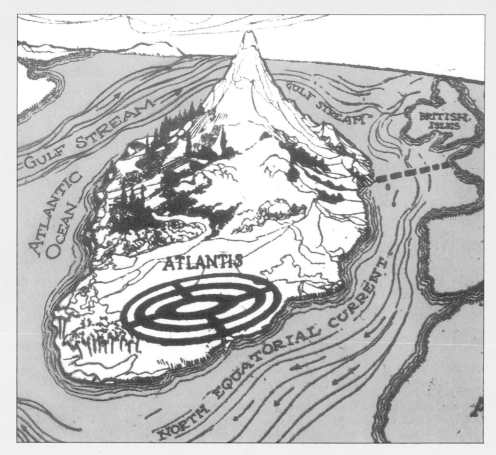

A huge volcanic eruption destroyed Thera in the Aegean Sea around 1520 B.C. (above), and the area of fallout was vast. The middle of Thera was submerged, leaving the small group of islands there today, one of which is Santorini. The buildings on Santorini bear the colors of the volcanic fallout – black, red, and white. These same colors were said by Plato to be typical of the buildings of Atlantis.

This map, presented at the beginning of the 20th century, turned out to be faked evidence of Atlantis' existence.

How do we know about the lives of ancient peoples?

We can find out about the lives of people who lived thousands of years ago in many different ways. Archeologists can dig up evidence from the ground consisting of things that our ancestors have made (artefacts), or even the remains of their bodies. We can also gain a good idea about how they lived by looking at the records that they kept of their own lives.

The first real records we have date from around 20,000 years ago. At that time early members of our own species, *Homo sapiens*, were painting wonderful pictures on the walls of their caves (see Question 65). These prehistoric paintings are a sort of cartoon strip of the lifestyles of those ancient humans. They show us, for instance, the animals that our ancestors hunted and fed on.

Some of the later cave paintings even show the hunting methods that they used: spears are easily told apart from bows and arrows in these detailed paintings. Even if archeologists had not found remains of weapons in the ground, these prehistoric picture records tell us without doubt what weapons were used.

From the time that written languages were developed, around 5,000 years ago (see Question 87), we have written records of ancient lives. By this stage, prehistoric time had turned into history. The records were carved on rock, pressed into wet clay which was then baked, or written in ink on hide or a sort of paper made out of strips of reed stalks (papyrus). They tell us much about the lives of Ancient Egyptians, for example – details about battles, the families of kings, the building of temples, the numbers of farm animals owned, or the extent of their territories.

Before written records existed, or in cultures where there are none surviving, our knowledge has had to come from whatever can be dug out of the ground. One source is the artefacts that ancient peoples made or used – their pots, their tools, and their weapons, as well as their buildings.

The types of buildings that our ancestors made can tell us how advanced their societies were. To build a hut of sticks, stones, and hides does not need much organization. But it takes tens of

thousands of organized workers and some sort of central government to plan and carry out the construction of a vast stone pyramid, or a complicated water transport system for irrigating fields over a huge area.

Even the kinds of garbage found in digs near human buildings from the past can tell us a surprising amount about the lives those people lived. Shells, bones, and fragments of old seeds can show exactly what shellfish, fish, animals, and crops the people were eating when the garbage pits were made, and even whether they were eating food from wild or cultivated sources. And pollen from flowers, as well as seeds and insect remains found on a dig can tell archeologists what sort of climate the people were living in when these buried remains were first deposited.

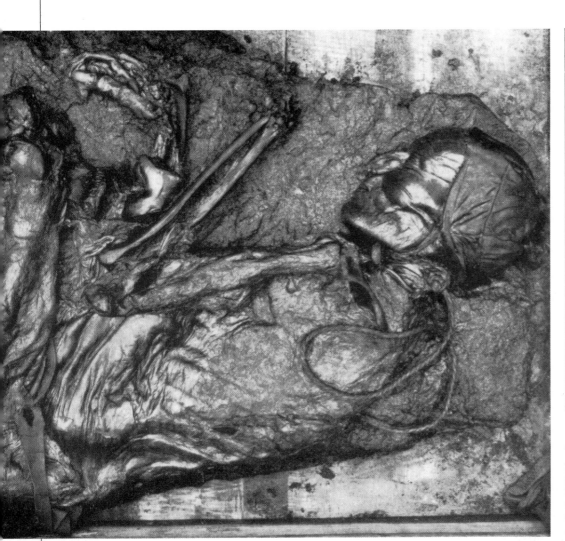

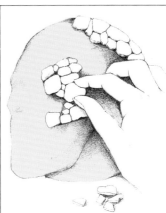

Piecing together broken bones found in a dig is like making a 3D jigsaw puzzle; it is the job of specialists. Here an "anatomist" arranges pieces of skull bone around the clay model of a head. The soft clay can be reshaped to match the curves of the skull as it is assembled.

Tollund Man was garrotted 2,000 years ago and thrown into a peat bog in Denmark. The peat tanned his skin like leather, and it is still possible to see detailed facial characteristics and to make out what he was wearing.

What can human remains tell us?

The most common prehistoric human remains are bones and teeth, which do not rot away like human flesh, and they can tell us a good deal.

By careful measurement and examination, specialists can work out the age and the sex of human bones found in digs. As children get older, there is a definite sequence of changes that takes place in the "solidification" of the bone ends. There is also, of course, a series of changes from baby teeth to adult teeth. Some parts of the human skeleton, for instance the pelvis, can be used to tell a woman's bones from a man's.

In unusual circumstances, conditions in the ground can stop decay almost completely, and it is sometimes possible to find human bodies of great age that are incredibly well preserved. The special conditions may be exceptionally dry, extremely cold, or due to a lack of oxygen in the ground where the corpse is buried.

In the dry atmosphere of sealed rock tombs, well-protected mummies of 3,000 or more years old may show almost lifelike features when unwrapped. And almost 2,500 years ago, in the Pazyryk Valley in central Asia, the dead bodies of chiefs were placed in icy tombs. These cold storage conditions meant that when the bodies of these chieftains were excavated they still had intact skin, covered in skilfully drawn animal tattoos.

Remains have been found from about 2,000 years ago, in both Denmark and Ireland, of people who had been thrown into peat bogs after being strangled. Due to the acidic conditions of the bogs, their skin is exceptionally well preserved.

What does an archeologist do?

Archeologists are here excavating an early Roman fort in the north of England. The photograph shows only one corner of the vast excavation site.

Archeologists organize and carry out "digs" at sites where ancient people once lived. They also record all the information that comes out of the dig.

In past centuries, digs were rather amateur affairs; they were adventures, whose main object was the hunt for treasure of some sort. This meant that, very often, the top layers of ground were rapidly upturned and thrown away in an effort to get to the older layers underneath. There was a great risk that valuable objects and information were missed or thrown away, and no proper records of the dig could be made. Nowadays, great care is taken to gather every possible scrap of information from a site. Archeology is today a very precise and scientific activity.

The place where a dig should begin can be decided either from records of the past which describe the location of an interesting town, palace, or temple. Alternatively, it is necessary to look at the present landscape for clues about what might lie underneath. This may involve the use of aerial photography to look for tell-tale markings on the ground, or the use of metal detectors. Sometimes objects come

to light accidentally, either when the foundations for a modern building are being dug, or by deep plowing by farmers.

Once the site has been chosen, the digging itself takes place systematically, layer by layer. Detailed maps are made, and records kept of the objects found in each layer, before that layer is removed and work begun on the one beneath it. Some ancient materials, like stones, pottery, glass, and most metals, survive well underground, and these – as well as the disturbed earth layers – reveal to the archeologist what was going on at each layer that is uncovered.

On the other hand, organic objects made of wood and hides rot away quickly, except in special circumstances where rotting is delayed (for instance, in very dry conditions). But even when they have rotted, they may leave spaces, colorations, or marks in the soil, which can be recorded.

The careful mapping, and the photographs taken of objects found in different areas and at different depths in the dig, prove essential when it comes to reconstructing the history of the site from the remains that have been found there.

How can the age of things found in a dig be worked out?

There are many ways in which the ancient objects found in an archeological dig can be dated. Usually, several different methods are used together, so that a reliable estimate of real age can be made.

The most obvious way of dating things, particularly artefacts, or objects made by ancient people, is to compare the details of the way they are made, and the style of decoration, with other objects that have been found before and have already been accurately dated. This is especially useful for items like coins, statues, pottery, and wine jars. Sometimes, with even a small fragment of pottery, it is possible to tell from its shape, color, and the patterns on it, exactly where it was made and when.

There is another scientific way for working out the age of pottery, called "thermoluminescence" dating. When pottery is fired in a kiln, the crystals in the clay take in some energy which becomes "locked" into the pottery while it stays at ordinary temperatures. But once the pottery is heated to a high temperature again, some of this energy leaks out as light. This can be picked up and measured by sensitive instruments and, from the amount of light given out, experts can tell how long ago the pot was first placed in a kiln and baked.

Tree rings can be used to date old wooden objects very reliably. The patterns of wide and narrow tree rings are much the same in all trees over the same time period, in a particular part of the world. It is therefore possible to build up a "library" of ancient tree rings which enable the age of any wooden object to be dated with, sometimes, extraordinary accuracy. A sequence of recognizable ring patterns stretching back about 8,000 years has now been worked out.

In 1990, for instance, scientists using tree ring data were able to say that a wooden causeway – called the Sweet Track – laid across a swamp in Somerset in southern England had been built from timber felled in the winter and early spring of 3807–3806 B.C. – nearly 6,000 years ago!

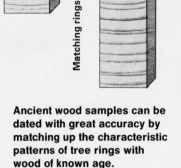

Matching rings

Matching rings

Ancient wood samples can be dated with great accuracy by matching up the characteristic patterns of tree rings with wood of known age.

In North America the tree ring method of dating has been used with bristlecone pines. These trees can live nearly 5,000 years.

GLOSSARY

You may find it useful to know the meanings of some of these scientific words when reading the questions and answers in this book.

Ammonite An extinct group of sea-living relatives of today's squids and octopuses. The ammonites had coiled hard shells, inside which a soft animal with tentacles lived.

Amphibian Animals like frogs, newts, and salamanders. Amphibians are cold-blooded backboned creatures with soft skins without scales. Most lay eggs in water which hatch into swimming tadpoles with gills. The tadpoles then change into the air-breathing adult forms of amphibian.

Archeologist A scientist who digs up the remains of ancient peoples and their buildings and belongings from under the ground or who finds them under the sea. These finds are then used to get a clear idea of how those people lived long ago.

Artefact Anything made or constructed by people. Pottery, weapons, paintings, and buildings that are found in archeological digs are all artefacts.

Astronomer A scientist who studies everything that can be seen in space—moons, planets, the Sun, and other stars and galaxies.

Atom The minute "particles" of which everything in the Universe is made. All atoms have a central nucleus.

Bacteria One-celled organisms—some of the simplest living things known on Earth. They may live independent lives or depend for existence on some other living creature. Many bacteria live in our bodies, and some of them cause disease.

Cell The basic unit of life. The simplest living plants and animals are made of one single cell. A complex creature such as a tree or a human contains millions of cells.

Epidemic A rapid and severe outbreak of a disease. An epidemic is usually caused when a new type of germ gets into a population of people or animals that have little or no immunity to the germ.

Evolution The changes that slowly happen to living things over many generations. Through evolution, animals and plants become more successful in the conditions in which they find themselves living. Sometimes as they change (or evolve) the creatures become so different that they become new species.

Galaxy A huge collection of stars, gas, and dust. Stars are made in a galaxy, and a galaxy may contain more than a billion stars of different ages. The Sun, our own star, is part of the Milky Way galaxy.

Gene The part of the cell of an animal or plant responsible for passing on characteristics from one generation to another. The genes of an organism are responsible for the way it looks, works, and behaves.

Geological A word used to describe things which have to do with the rocks out of which the Earth's crust is built. A **geological age** is one of the long periods of our planet's past, lasting many millions of years. The beginning and end of each age is decided on the basis of the layers of rocks laid down at those times in the past, and the fossils found in them.

Hunter-gatherers People, like some rain-forest tribes today, who live a very primitive life. They do not farm or build permanent places to live. They move all the time, hunting animals for food and collecting wild plants to eat. Until 10,000 years ago all people were hunter-gatherers.

Invertebrates Animals that do not have a backbone. Most species of animals have bodies like this. Insects, worms, spiders, snails, starfish, corals, and many other sorts of animals are all invertebrates.

Mammal A backboned, warm-blooded animal with a covering of fur or hair. Mammals feed their young with milk from mammary glands and most give birth to large offspring which have developed for a long time in the mother's womb.

Mausoleum A temple where the tomb of a great ruler is placed.

Microbe A microscopic organism, but especially a bacterium that causes disease.

Molecule A combination of atoms. A water molecule contains two hydrogen atoms and one oxygen atom, and is symbolized as H_2O.

Oxygen The gas in the atmosphere that most animals and plants need in order to gain energy. It is a colorless, tasteless gas that makes up about 21 per cent of the air.

Paleontologist A scientist who finds and studies fossils. The fossils can be used to understand what long-extinct creatures looked like and how they lived.

Pharoah A king or other great ruler in Ancient Egypt.

Plate tectonics The process which explains the behavior of the Earth's crust. The crust is thought to be divided into eight enormous plates or "rafts," which are in constant motion, either toward or away from each other. Where plates come together, as at the San Andreas Fault in California, earthquakes commonly occur.

Race A group of living things which are all in the same species but whose creatures differ in some ways from those in the other races, or sub-species. They may differ in things like size, color, and body patterning. Races in the same species can breed with one another.

Reptile A backboned animal like a lizard, snake, crocodile, tortoise or dinosaur. Reptiles are cold-blooded, usually have dry, scaly skins and breathe air. They lay eggs with tough leathery skins which hatch into young that look like small versions of their parents.

Sedimentary Describes rocks made in the distant past by the laying down of fine material like mud or sand by the action of water or wind. These layers of sediments—as they are called—in the end get pressed down and hardened into rocks. Chalk, limestone, and sandstone are all types of sedimentary rocks.

Species All the living things of a particular type that can breed with one another are called a species. Not all creatures in a species will look exactly the same though. Species are often divided up into smaller groups which share some differences in the way they look or behave— these groups are called sub-species or races. Despite the differences, the various races and sub-species in one species can all breed with one another.

Tropical The hot, wet regions of the world around the equator.

Vertebrates Animals that have a backbone. Most of the large animals in the world have bodies like this. Fish, amphibians, reptiles, birds, and mammals, including humans, are all invertebrates.

Index

Page numbers in **bold** type indicate illustrations

Acknowledgments

Artwork by
Steve Kirk
Paul Richardson
Ed Stuart
Ian Bott
Colin Newman
Vana Haggerty
Malcolm Ellis
Stan North
Andrew Robinson
Andrew Wheatcroft
Kevin Hicks
Christine Wilson
John Hutchinson
Graham Allen
Michael Woods
Karen Daws

Photographs by
6 British Museum/Michael Holford; 9 Ronald Royer/Science Photo Library; 12 Dr J.D. Picket-Heaps/Science Photo Library; 13 Paul Shambroom/Science Photo Library; 18/19 Sinclair Stammers/Science Photo Library; 19 Vaughan Fleming; 22/23 Peter Scoones/ Seaphot; 27 John Durham/ Science Photo Library; 28 Sinclair Stammers/Imperial College; 28/29 E. Hummel/Zefa Picture Library; 35 Sinclair Stammers/Science Photo Library; 37 British Museum (Natural History); 41 Dr Guiseppe Mazza; 45 Topham Picture Source; 49 R.I.M. Campbell/Bruce Coleman; 54 Sarah Errington/The Hutchison Library; 58t Bryan & Cherry Alexander; 58c Penny Tweedie/Impact Photos; 58b John Bulmer; 59t Brian Boyd/Colorific!; 59b Aspect Picture Library; 60/61 Michael Holford; 62 Robert Harding Picture Library; 65 The Horniman Museum, London; 66/67 Biophoto Associates/Science Photo Library; 70/71 British Museum/ Michael Holford; 72 Sally & Richard Greenhill; 74 British Museum/Michael Holford; 76 J. Alex Langley/Aspect Picture Library; 78 William MacQuitty; 79 William MacQuitty; 80/81 British Museum/Michael Holford; 81 British Museum/Michael Holford; 82/83 Zefa Picture Library; 83 Fay Godwin; 86 John Wright/Aspect Picture Library; 87 Reflejo/Susan Griggs Agency; 88/89 Topham Picture Source; 90 GSF Picture Library